Rim-'t'yre
and the
STONES OF TIME

*Nina,
Discover the magic
in every ride!
Mitzy Tait-Zeller*

MITZY TAIT-ZELLER

Rim-Fyre and the Stones of Time

Copyright © 2013 by Mitzy Tait-Zeller

All rights reserved. No part of this book may be reproduced or transmitted in any form or by any means electronic or mechanical including photocopying or my any information storage or retrieval system without permission in writing from the author. This is a work of fiction. While references may be made to actual places or events, the names, characters, incidents and locations within are from the author's imagination and are not a resemblance to actual living or dead persons, businesses or events. Any similarity is coincidental.

ISBN-13: 978-1484852163
ISBN-10: 1484852168

Front cover photo and author photo on back cover by Sheila Stienley. www.sheilastienleyart.com

Cover design by Heather Upchurch from Expert Subjects. Interior design by Expert Subjects.

To all the horses that have carried me

on this journey called life. ~ Mitzy

Contents

Chapter 1 – The Journey Begins 1
Chapter 2 – 1887 11
Chapter 3 – Joan's Story 27
Chapter 4 – Dreaming 43
Chapter 5 – A Plan 52
Chapter 6 – Derek, 2012 65
Chapter 7 – Travels 78
Chapter 8 – Big Medicine 97
Chapter 9 – Interrogations, 2012 106
Chapter 10 – Pelipa, Lover of Horses 110
Chapter 11 – An Eagle and a Gift 116
Chapter 12 – Troubles 122
Chapter 13 – Painstaking Journey 131
Chapter 14 – Return to Swift Current 141
Chapter 15 –Visions 152
Chapter 16 – Thanksgiving and a Job 171
Chapter 17 – Magic Stones 192
Chapter 18 – Commitment 204
Chapter 19 – Hunter's Moon 211
Chapter 20 – Home 220

Acknowledgements 227

ONE
The Journey Begins

The journey of a thousand miles begins with a single step.
~ Lao Tzu

The morning sun gleamed on his dark chestnut coat. He turned one more circle before bending his knees and hocks for a roll in the dirt. His flowing flaxen mane flopped onto the ground as he rolled over onto his back for a good scratch. Back and forth he rolled stirring up the dust, grinding it into his coat. Ah, that felt so good. Back up on his belly, the mature stallion stretched out his fore limbs, rocked his body forward and upward in a sitting position then pushed his powerful hind limbs beneath him to stand. A full body shake vibrated most of the dirt off his now dusty coat to float softly back to earth. The healthy coat still shone through the dust with his abundant mane draped down both sides of his neck. He shook his magnificent head to adjust his lengthy forelock.

Snorting loudly he proclaimed his 'harrumph' that he was king here.

The sound of a closing door drew the stallion's attention. He could hear her footfalls coming his way. With ears perked forward he stood at the gate and watched her round the corner. He nickered his familiar greeting which was then followed by a chorus of whinnies erupting in unison from behind the barn.

With a smile in her voice she greeted him in return, "Hello Rim-Fyre, I'm happy to see you too, you gorgeous boy." She looked him in the eye and approached the fence to pet him. He turned his head to snap at her as her hand came up to touch his velvety soft muzzle. Just as quickly she moved her hand out of range, "None of that now. Be nice!" Her tone was firm and lowered. "Nice. I want to pet the pretty horse." Again she brought her hand up to pet him and this time he stood and let her stroke his nose. "Good boy." She then turned to walk into the barn to get a halter and lead shank.

To keep his mouth busy, Serena offered Rim-Fyre a treat at the gate which he lipped up with great enthusiasm. His antics this morning were a sure sign that he was bored and needed to get out for some exercise. As he thoughtfully chewed on the preferred treat, she opened the gate and looped the halter over his nose. He flipped his muzzle to the side to make a grab at her which was expertly blocked by her bony elbow. She had to straighten out his thick tangle of mane and forelock to secure the rope halter on his massive head.

Another open mouthed advance was made before she could open the gate. Again, the advance was blocked with rhythmic pressure of her hands directed at his eyes, waving her hand until he backed six or seven steps away from her. "Sorry pal, not today you don't!" *Not any other day either*, she thought to herself. Serena took up the end of her lead shank and swung it in a circular motion toward his hind quarters to get him to yield to the pressure. Rim-Fyre was not about to let the shank hit him. His master was asking for something in a calm manner and he would respond as his natural instinct and training had taught him. She asked him for a few small circles in his paddock before leading him back to the gate and safely into the barn.

Shadows began to recede as the sun peaked over the tops of the trees in front of the barn. It was going to be a lovely autumn day, perfect for that ride that both Rim-Fyre and Serena needed.

Gently nickering 'her-her-her', Rim-Fyre stood proudly waiting as he heard her rustling grain in the feed room. Serena smiled as she walked towards him with the feeder and some grain. "I love it when you call me her-her-her. I'm sure that's my name in horse language because all the horses call me that."

Rim-Fyre backed up so that she could place the feeder and dump the oats into it. When she stepped back he plunged his masculine head into the feeder but took his time gently lipping up every oat and thoughtfully chewing them.

Serena soon returned with brushes to curry him, followed by fast action flicking of the dandy brush to remove the dirt he ground into his coat during that glorious roll earlier. Within minutes, Rim-Fyre was brushed and gleaming once again while he leisurely enjoyed the last of his rolled oats. Five minutes had not passed before Rim-Fyre was saddled and ready for that much needed ride. Serena stood with his bridle, calmly stroking his neck while he finished the last mouthful of oats. Another cookie was offered and his bridle was positioned with gentle expert hands.

Garbed entirely in shades of brown other than her blue jeans and lined jean jacket, Serena was layered up for the day. The air was still cool this morning and layers could be shed later as the day warmed. When riding Rim she never knew which bush he might decide to walk through, so she put on her chinks and grabbed her stock whip on her way out the door.

Rim-Fyre pranced as she led him north of the barn to an open area to mount. Serena checked the girth for tightness and placed the braided leather reins over his neck. She wiggled the saddle horn and set her left foot in the stirrup to mount. Rim-Fyre swung his head around to nip her in the backside, grazing the conch on her chinks as she swung up into the saddle. "Here now!" she growled at him.

Without daily riding and interaction, Serena would have to start at square one with Rim-Fyre to prove to him that she was a good leader and would not be dominated by his behaviour.

She asked Rim-Fyre to back up a half dozen steps before turning him to ride out of the yard. He walked with purpose and felt a mile high. His ears were perked forward as he strutted ahead with all the pride he could muster. He was collected and gorgeous, his thick neck bulging from her viewpoint. She relaxed the reins in her hands a few inches and he broke into a smooth jog which quickly became a posting trot. The pace increased, they were now at the lane out of the yard and headed toward the main road. Rim-Fyre broke into a lope which became a hand gallop and then the rocking motion of his crow-hopping began and took them all the way to the end of the lane. Serena easily sat his crow-hopping and revelled in all that robust energy. The gallop continued left onto the main road when Rim-Fyre kicked out his hind quarters in a hard buck. She pulled him to a stop, backed him up and made him stand for a few seconds before they continued. He stepped out at a walk but was so full of energy, wanting to quickly increase speed. Serena wanted to let him run some of the fire out of his system, too, so that they could get onto the best part of the ride. Once again, jog, lope and run as hard as he could, buck, stop, back up and continue. They made their way down the road for more than a mile in exactly that fashion. Serena was glad there weren't any vehicles on the road that morning to watch this spectacle. They rode south and west with the road then another turn south onto a main grid road to cross the black steel frame bridge that went over the Swift Current Creek.

Her plan was to follow the creek from the other side of the bridge along the hills of native prairie grass so that she could see the farm from the other side. She loved riding in the hills there near the water. It was like stepping back in time when the land was free and unbroken. If she was lucky, she would see geese and ducks which would begin flocking for migration soon. Often a few white-tailed deer could be seen while riding along the creek. If startled, they would jump high out of the bushes with white tails flagging in the air as they ran off in search of another safer place.

Rim-Fyre had exerted some of that pent-up energy and now walked calmly across the bridge. The water was shallow beneath the black steel frame and spanned more than fifty feet at this point. Reining him to the left, they walked onto the dry prairie grass along the creek bank. Sage poked its head through the tall grasses interspersed here and there to wave its blue-ish tint and scent on the breeze. The smell of sage as they passed was faint but when brushed against, its pungent aroma would envelop them. The sky was as blue as a robin's egg in spring, dotted only with a few white clouds that resembled sheep. Serena basked in the sun's warming rays and enjoyed the scenery spread out vastly before her. The fields all reddish brown with the dryness of harvest over and green grass poked up from the dry prairie wool where there was more moisture. Small bushes near the water's edge took on shades of orange and yellow, where leaves still clung stubbornly to their place on the branches. Fall was evident all around them. An occasional crisp, dry branch of sage brush crunched under Rim-Fyre's large oval hooves. Various sized bleached grey rocks scattered hither and yon displayed multicolored lichen in varying shades of green and reddish brown. It was truly a picture perfect setting in which to enjoy a ride.

As they neared the creek, the sun glinted brightly off the rippling water running over rocks peaking from the surface. In other places, it barely rippled in the minimal breeze. Serena could not focus on the reflective water for too long, it was bright and burned her eyes.

The ground was firm as they made their way eastward the way the creek curved. It would turn northward on a winding course that would take it more than thirty miles to empty into the South Saskatchewan River. A smooth jog took them a quarter mile along the creek before she signaled him to walk. He picked his way with purpose through the deep grass and down through the ravine that broke from the hill top and made its cutting way down to the water's edge. Now on the hill tops high above the creek, they could see the farm in the distance. Rim-Fyre neighed a greeting in recognition of home, hoping for a whinny in reply. The scenery enveloped them and they became a part of the prairie landscape. Although Serena was sure that Rim-Fyre's dark chestnut coat stuck out even though his flaxen mane and tail blended with the prairie grass and harvest hues. Even more rocks stuck out from the grass on this part of the hills. She turned Rim-Fyre off the crest of the hill and closer to the water once again. They made their way down the hill, skirting the now grass-filled depression of what once was a buffalo wallow more than a century past. Often, when Serena would ride in the hills that wend their way along the creek, she would see the deep depressions scattered along or near the hill tops not far from the water. She was sure that at one time this must have been home to many buffalo. Briefly she mourned the loss of the buffalo, recalling that several years ago conservationists released a herd of prairie bison in The Grasslands National Park, which was eighty miles south of Swift Current. Apparently the herd was doing well and had increased in numbers. Serena hoped to go down there someday with her family to catch a glimpse of them roaming peaceably in their natural habitat.

A flat area in the bottom of the shelter of hills warranted a lope. Rim-Fyre obliged her leg cues and gave a smooth flowing gait that felt like a favorite rocking chair to Serena. The level area took them right to the opposite bank from the farm which looked so peaceful, surrounded by trees that sheltered the house and shop from the westerly winds. The mares and fillies ran down to the fence line in their pasture south of the house and whinnied a greeting to them. Rim-Fyre bugled back. They stood quietly for a few moments and drank in the scene of the farm. Rim-Fyre took in a sharp breath through his flared nostrils and let it out slowly, relaxing as he did so. He, too, was taking in the scene and scents around them.

With leg and rein pressure Serena asked him to turn on his haunches and go back the way they came. Her plan was to take Rim-Fyre further south along the railroad tracks that were east of the creek and on another tour further west to cross a different bridge before riding home. It would be an eleven mile round trip, of which they had only come four. The creek was on their right with the hills looming loftily to their left. Serena gave Rim-Fyre his head and turned him toward the hills. Off he bounded with instant power, sinking his hard hooves into the grass beneath them. She sat on him effortlessly as he reached longer strides galloping up the base of the hill and to the top. With his mane now whipping in her face, she laughed with sheer exhilaration. Serena got a funny feeling in her stomach as he leaped over the hill at its rise, then slowed to a trot and a walk. She exhaled a lungful of air as if she had been holding her breath. *Damn that felt good!*

They went south, Rim-Fyre choosing each step around stones now strewn helter-skelter in the grass. Serena suspected that the lichen covered stones had been there for a long time.

Rim-Fyre was responding to her aids. Gently, she asked for another lope which he obliged willingly. They were in their element as they loped down the hill slope and up the next with the momentum increasing slightly as his hoof falls beat out a staccato rhythm down the next slope. The grass was deep this year and rocks were everywhere. Unprepared, Serena found herself surrounded by a brilliant flash of white light as Rim-Fyre jumped an invisible barrier that she was unable to see. Then Rim halted and stood as still as a statue.

Temporarily disoriented and feeling somewhat nauseous after the blinding light Serena dismounted. When the feeling passed, she checked Rim-Fyre over and he seemed fine too.

What had happened there? Here? Serena looked down at the grass and it appeared shorter somehow. They were standing in what appeared to be a circle of stones placed strategically and with purpose. She looked up and scanned the horizon from their position, it was familiar but different now and she couldn't readily put her finger on what it was. Rim-Fyre nuzzled Serena's hand gently, his eye extraordinarily kind, then he raised his muzzle to the breeze and let out a grievous whinny, the likes of which she had never heard.

Rim-Fyre and the Stones of Time

What happened when Rim-Fyre jumped? What was that flash? Were they dead? A sudden cold fear gripped Serena's chest, feeling as though she might suffocate. Rim-Fyre stepped on Serena's foot, instinctively she pushed him away. It hurt. *That was a good sign, wasn't it? Pain meant she wasn't dead, unless she was in hell, that is.*

TWO
1887

Time is the longest distance between two places.
~ Tennessee Williams

Now what? Serena made a mental note of the rock circle in which they now stood, maybe this was important. She had always been known for her photographic memory and hoped that it wouldn't fail her now. From the rocks, to the creek which now seemed lower, more of a trickle than it had been before 'the incident', to the open grassland that surrounded them completely. No more were the harvested fields of lentils on the east side of the hills where they stood. The eastern horizon seemed different too, she knew there was a railroad track just over there but the landscape signified otherwise. To her right and west she looked and it, too, was all native prairie, no more hay land across the creek and no irrigation pipes scattered in that field. Most shocking of all when she looked back from the path they just came, her farm and home were nowhere to be seen. No barn, no horses, no house, no trees, only shrubbery along the banks of the creek with open prairie to the west and no visible roads. Serena's chest constricted tighter and threatened to cut off her air, adrenaline coursed from her lower back down the back of her legs.

"Rim-Fyre, where the hell are we?"

He nipped her pocket with purpose, not malice. It was to tell her to get on him and together they would go look. With Serena back in the saddle, Rim-Fyre wanted to show her what he knew. Now it was gloomy and overcast. They neared the place where they skirted the buffalo wallow earlier, Rim-Fyre stopped and waited for Serena to notice. She squeezed her legs against his sides to continue but he stood stubbornly in place. She had been too wrapped up in her own thoughts until she looked closely at the ground around them, there was obviously something there she was supposed to see. It took a few moments for her brain to register what her eyes were seeing. There wasn't any grass growing in the buffalo wallow, it was a dry dust bowl and now she could see that several wallows dotted the hills around them. This was an important clue and Rim-Fyre was trying to communicate with her.

Serena's throat constricted in that familiar way right before she would cry, leaning down onto Rim-Fyre's neck she hugged him as tears threatened. "Oh Rim-Fyre, where are we and why are we here?" A deep breath escaped her trying to still the tears that had not fallen, "How are we going to get home?" She was pretty sure he didn't know the answer but he was all she had at the moment. He turned his stately head and nuzzled her knee in what she could only assume was consolation. That small gesture brought her to her senses and she sat up straight once again. "All right then, lead the way, show me what you know." She had a feeling she was going to be talking more to Rim-Fyre than she ever had in her life. That is, if she wasn't dead. Serena still wasn't sure whether this was what death was or not, an alternate hell maybe?

Rim-Fyre walked on through the sea of prairie grass. Serena had never seen her home surroundings look like this and yet the hill lines and the creek were still all there. No fences though, old or new. The neighbor's house no longer overlooked the creek bank on the opposite side of the water and when they rounded the bend, there was no Black Bridge or sign of a road there at all. It was as if they had stepped back in time.

Wait a minute! Stepped back in time! That's it, but how? And how far back in time did they come? Again the question rang like church bells in her brain, *how are we going to get home? Was this an alternate hell? Were they dead? If not, why were they here?* Too many questions flooded her brain, it was on overload now.

Rim-Fyre continued walking but veered southwest towards what looked like a wooden grain shed near the spot where the old Skyline Ranch had been. A few shrubs were nearby the shed and what looked like a small number of livestock in the distance. As they approached the shed, the creek below the area came into view and Serena could see two people there. *I guess this will be the test to see if we are dead or not.*

Rim-Fyre kept his pace to a generous walk which covered the ground quickly but was not hurried or proud. By all appearances the two men she came upon were fairly young. They were filling buckets of water and fastening them onto what looked like a neck yoke or something for oxen, so that they could carry them over their shoulders. Rim-Fyre ignored the horses that she could see now with their heads raised in the distance. The horses called out and the men looked up from their duties.

One of the men walked toward her. He hollered out, "Good day to you."

They walked closer until Rim-Fyre stopped at what he felt was a safe distance. "Good day." Serena replied with all the assurance of an ant. She wasn't sure if her voice sounded right or not.

"I'm Ed and that's my brother Al," he said pointing to the other man that was now walking to stand beside him. "That's some fine lookin' hoss you got yerself there, young lad."

"Good day to you." *Young lad? Wow, he thought she was young and a man at that!* Serena laughed inwardly but did not manifest it externally at all. She supposed from the way she was dressed, with her short hair under her hat, no makeup and her gravelly voice from being an ex-smoker, she could be mistaken for a young lad. Maybe she could make this work for her somehow.

She overheard Al say to his brother Ed, "Educated feller by the looks of it."

"Thank you, name's Derek. I had a wreck here a day or so ago and knocked myself clean out of my head, lost track of time. You wouldn't happen to know what day it is, would you?" she asked hopefully.

Al answered her question, "It's the first day of fall, year of our Lord 1887."

Serena choked on, "Excuse me?!"

"Ya deaf, boy? I said it's September 21st, year of our Lord 1887!" Al shouted at her.

Rim-Fyre shifted beneath her and backed up a step as she regained her composure. "It appears I have lost more than a day or two from banging my head. Thank you gentlemen, I should be on my way." She tipped her hat in farewell.

As Ed walked toward them, Rim-Fyre eyed him warily and backed up step for advancing step. The man stopped, realizing he was making no advance on her horse. "Sorry, didn't mean to spook yer horse," he apologized. "If'n yer fixin' on goin' ta town, it's that way," he said pointing towards what Serena knew to be the location of the city.

She glanced the way he pointed. "Thank you for your time gentlemen, I think that's exactly where I'll be heading next."

"Oh we're not gentlemen," Ed offered, "we're just reg'lar folk." The 'folk' ended abruptly as his brother Al elbowed him in the ribs.

"One thing before you leave," Al interjected, "where'd you get that horse and what is he?"

Serena felt she better be careful what information she offered these men if she really was in 1887, the first Canadian Stud Book was just written in 1886. "This here is one of those Quebecer horses, brought him all the way from out east. Tough as nails, is what I heard, so I took a chance. He hasn't let me down yet," she said turning Rim-Fyre towards town. "Thanks again boys."

She waved as Rim-Fyre walked off across the field. The brothers waved their farewells.

Rim-Fyre loped until they reached the creek. The water was shallow so Rim-Fyre stepped right in leaning his head down for a big drink. Serena slid her hand forward with the reins on his neck and allowed him his fill. When he proceeded, he seemed to take great merriment in splashing as he walked through the knee deep, cold water. Rim-Fyre went up the other bank with ease as they continued on what appeared to be a deer trail. Serena turned him east towards their farm location. They crested the hill and scanned the valley below them. There was no farm nestled in the bottom along the creek bank. The vastness of the native prairie spread before them like a sea of grass, sage interspersed here and there. Home was now a foreign wilderness.

They galloped across the arid prairie towards what was once their home, Rim-Fyre again called out his grievous whinny. His cry broke her heart, as a tear escaped and rolled gently down her cheek, leaving her longing for home.

Suddenly Serena remembered her cell phone in her jacket pocket. Grabbing it out of her pocket she flipped it open. It gave a time and date, the time was now 1:30 in the afternoon and the date said September 21st, 2012. She quickly did the math. They had travelled back in time 125 years, but why? She closed her phone and shut it off. She had no idea how long it would last and knew there wouldn't be any cell service for at least 100 and some years.

Rim-Fyre ambled now in remorse to the creek bank where the farm had been. Maybe if they sat there for a while they could figure out a way to get home in the next day or so. She dismounted and walked the length of the creek where their farm should be, in their time. It was wild prairie with a few bushes scattered here and there near the water's edge. Serena sat on the bank across from the hill where they had been nearly two hours ago, looking at their farm. Now she gazed at the hill across the creek and how it appeared 125 years ago - same but different. Rim-Fyre stood nearby, she still held his reins but he didn't try to pull nor step on her in any way. His whole demeanor had changed since the incident.

She was glad she was sitting when the realization of the whole scenario hit her like a brick to the head. No home, no house, no barn, it was going to freeze tonight, no bed to sleep in, no family to greet. In only a few short hours the kids would be home from school and mom wasn't going to be there to greet them or hug and kiss them. The constricting panic gripped her like a vise and threatened to strangle her. She dropped her head to her hands and cried with grief over the loss of everything she held dear. More than her own grief she mourned for Jess and Cole, how broken her children would be over their mom's disappearance. And Derek, her beloved Derek, what would he do? She continued crying as the tears ran freely. She didn't know how long she wept, was it minutes or hours?

Rim-Fyre nudged her shoulder, took a bite of grass near where she sat and nudged her again. She wiped her eyes with the back of her hands and used the sleeve of her jacket to wipe her runny nose. "Alright horse, where are we going now?" She asked standing up. Rim-Fyre nosed the stirrup. She looked at him, really looked at him and took his muzzle in her hands while looking into his eyes. They just looked at each other but he made no move to try to grab her or her clothing with his teeth. "Alright, let's go." She gently let go of his muzzle, placed the reins over his neck and stepped into the saddle. Once she had her foot in the other stirrup he began walking towards where she knew Swift Current should be. There were only deer trails to follow up and over a small hill then across the bottom of a large open area and up the big hill south of the city.

It was only a few miles to town but the landscape they rode over made it seem longer, Serena had never been so aware of her surroundings until that moment. She glanced to the east and saw there was no longer a railroad track on the other side of the creek, the hills she had ridden in as a kid were now unmarked by the passage of the tracks. It was breathtakingly beautiful with a few deer scattered here and there. There was no city water dam and treatment plant flooding the low spots. The cut banks where the creek cut into the hill long ago were not the eroded soft dirt she knew but were instead clear, ragged cuts in the dirt that resembled a small canyon. It was breathtaking.

They were not really rushing but Serena's stomach was growling. How long was it since she had eaten? They topped the hill and stood at the top of the cut banks. Perhaps Serena was expecting something else but only more open prairie greeted them and the hill that was once filled with residential homes was native grass. One lone house occupied the top of what was known as Oman Hill. A windmill stood beside the house and a few straggly trees were there. A lean-to shed and a small corral were behind and to the east of the house. A wagon wheel rutted trail led from the house down the northeast side of the hill to where she knew her son's school to be. There was no school, only more open grass dotted with sage and the odd bush. This was a time long before all that she knew.

Rim-Fyre veered toward the house. Serena figured she better stick to her story of having hit her head and lost her provisions. Maybe she could secure enough employment to get a meal. She was not opposed to hard work, she was farm raised.

Rim-Fyre walked to the hitching rail and fence in front of the house on the hill. Serena dismounted and a woman came out of the door to stand there obviously to speak to her from a distance. Serena presumed it was because she was a stranger and back then, er now, back now? Well either way, she was a stranger. She wrapped the reins of Rim-Fyre's bridle around the rail and walked part way to the house. Appearing like a man from the woman's perspective of things, she kept some distance so this woman wouldn't feel threatened by her presence.

She removed her hat to reveal her short brown hair. "Howdy ma'am," she offered. "My name's Derek."

"Howdy Mister Derek, what can I do fer ya?" she wrung her hands in the dishtowel she held.

"I had a wreck and hurt my head, lost some time and my provisions when I stumbled into the area here. I was wondering if you might tell me where I could get some work and a meal."

"Sorry Mister Derek, my name's Agnes Knight, Mister Knight is in town down the road a piece," she said pointing to the rail yard buildings downtown.

"Would you mind going down to the creek and getting me a little firewood from the dead trees down around the corner there," she pointed eastward. "I would fix you a sandwich and some coffee, if'n you'd do that for me."

"I most certainly would Mrs. Knight, thank you." When Serena sat in the saddle, Rim-Fyre sensed the urgency in her need for food and loped all the way to the creek where Mrs. Knight directed.

Sure enough, there was deadfall lying around on the ground, dry and ready to burn. Serena couldn't carry the wood and lead Rim-Fyre so she tied his reins to the saddle horn with enough slack to graze. He followed her back and then dipped his nose to the short dry grass in the yard while she carried the wood to the house. There were two steps up to the front porch which boasted two willow chairs, a small table and a wooden box for the wood where Serena set the armful of fire wood.

Mrs. Knight came out of the wooden screen door with her hands full, she had a plate heaped with food in one hand and a tin mug of steaming coffee in the other. She set down Serena's earnings on a small wooden table set between the chairs. She motioned her to have a seat in the far willow chair. Mrs. Knight was an average size woman, shorter than Serena but a little rounder in the bottom. It was hard to tell with her full skirts. Her dark brown hair was tied in a bun at the nape of her neck, wisps escaping around the contours of her oval face.

"Thank you for bringing me that wood, Mister Derek," she said settling herself in the other willow chair. "Please go ahead and eat, you look like you could use some meat on your bones, young feller."

Removing her hat, Serena bowed her head to give thanks in silence, picked up the plate and had a bite of the sandwich. It was one of the most delicious things she had eaten, homemade bread and butter, meat that had been cooked to perfection and a homemade sliced pickle added to the mix. Mrs. Knight had been very generous with the bread slices and the meat. It was perfect.

Serena set the empty plate back down on the small table and reached for the coffee cup. Up until now Mrs. Knight had been curiously watching Rim-Fyre graze in her yard, free and able to leave at any time he wanted to.

"Beautiful animal you have there," Mrs. Knight nodded toward Rim-Fyre. "I can't get over how well behaved your stallion is. Any other stallion would have run over to greet our horse behind the shed out back by now."

"Maybe it's because he's unsure of himself here," Serena offered as explanation.

Mrs. Knight shrugged in answer. "They might need some help in town. I know they have rooms down at the C.P.R. Dining Room. You could check there for some work."

Serena finished the mug of black coffee and set the cup down. "I'll run down there and ask around. Thank you very much for the sandwich and coffee, Mrs. Knight. Maybe I'll pass through this way again. Your hospitality is most appreciated."

Mrs. Knight eyed her skeptically which made Serena uncomfortable. "They might have use for you in town with your education, not too many well educated fellers other than the business folk around here. Tell them Mrs. Knight sent you."

"Thank you ma'am, I'll be sure to do that." She placed her hat back on as she walked down the steps to her waiting horse.

The time was nearing 4 o'clock as she tipped her hat to Mrs. Knight and asked Rim-Fyre for a lope down the hill towards the Canadian Pacific Railroad rail yard.

Rim-Fyre loped smoothly down the trail which led across the railroad tracks about a mile away. A handful of houses were dotted here and there, not the streets and avenues of residential buildings that Serena knew. There was a large round building to her right as she rode up the trail that she presumed to be 2nd Avenue S.E. in her day. Serena recalled her mom saying something about a round house that the C.P.R. used to turn the train engines around. It was demolished in the 1960's. There was no overpass over the two train tracks that were now before her either. She saw the Dining Room or C.P.R. Hotel up ahead of her and what appeared to be main street Swift Current across the dirt road north of it. There were a dozen or so buildings, businesses or homes that faced the rail yard. She stuck to the dirt path as she rode past a dozen tipis before crossing the tracks. On the north side of the C.P.R. Dining Room she found a hitching rail, watered Rim-Fyre in the trough there and tied him. Serena stroked him affectionately on the forehead and then made her way through the front doors of the building.

She saw her reflection in the dirty window of the wooden door, a bell clanging as she entered. Tables and chairs were off to her left and on the right was a high counter top with a shelf on the wall behind it. Several windows lined the far wall facing the train tracks. The building appeared empty. It wasn't long before she heard footfalls from a staircase behind the wall that backed the registration counter. A woman with a plain brown dress and white apron came from around the wall.

She called out a greeting, "Good Afternoon! Sorry for the delay, I just laid the baby down for a nap." That struck Serena in the chest and a lump formed in her throat. She was not at home today when her kids came home and she missed them terribly. Serena tried to hold it together and cleared her throat.

"Good Afternoon, do you have any sort of employment that I might do for a meal and a place to stay?" She asked hopefully. "I ran into some trouble a few days back and my provisions were taken. All I have left are the clothes on my back and my horse."

The curator of the dining room walked behind the counter and looked Serena in the eye. Serena had a flashback and this woman looked familiar but she couldn't place her. She felt completely judged once again under this woman's scrutiny.

"Where did you come from?" was demanded of Serena.

Serena was taken aback and felt as though this woman knew where she came from. Did this woman know she came from the future? The woman whose name she didn't yet know began walking around the counter to face her when Rim-Fyre began neighing wildly. Serena knew that call and headed right back through the door. Several men were now standing around Rim-Fyre who was snapping and kicking at the men to keep their distance. She ran to comfort her horse by pushing the men out of her way and away from her horse. They backed away as she approached Rim-Fyre's side and untied him. He relaxed a little but was still laying his ears back and making threats at the men who looked on. Serena felt completely out of place and wanted to run.

The woman from the C.P.R. Dining Room came out of the door. No one said anything, they were just staring at her and the horse. One of the men turned around to greet the woman. "Miss Joan, do you know this here young fella? Or is he giving you some trouble? We were just having a look at this fine horse of his when the horse went all crazy like."

Serena tried to commit all of the faces staring at her to memory. Some of them wore bowler hats, floppy farmer's hats, they all had brown or blue loose trousers and white shirts with what looked like suspenders and what appeared to be woolen coats with buttons. Some of the men had moustaches, some beards or both and they all appeared to be in their late twenties or mid-thirties. There was one older gentleman distinguished by his grey hair. None of these men appeared to be cowboys, perhaps they were business men or farmers.

"Now boys, I know my cousin here has a fancy horse and all. Came from down east, got his-self into some trouble and just made it here to find me. Now you all head on back to work and I'll be sure to introduce you to him tomorrow." She stated with confidence and a hint of humor. "Well, what are y'all waitin' for? Don't be gawkin' like chickens, go on!" She waved her arms and they slowly walked towards the buildings on the other side of the dirt road speaking in low tones amongst themselves.

When the men had dispersed to some distance and could no longer hear them, the woman walked over to Serena and Rim-Fyre who was now calm and quiet. "My name's Joan. Bring your horse to the barn at the side of the Dining Room here. We'll put him away and then have a coffee and chat at 'my' kitchen table." It was not a request or invitation but rather an order. Serena just nodded her head and followed her to the barn with Rim-Fyre in tow.

Minutes later, Rim-Fyre was unsaddled, haltered and tied in a stall with hay in the manger. Joan said nothing more to Serena, only pointed her finger to where she could hang her saddle while she forked hay to her horse. Serena removed her chinks and hung them over her saddle, then meekly followed Joan through the Dining Room door. She led the way around the wall and up the stairs to her family living quarters. There was a hall at the top of the stairs with several doorways that led to different rooms. Serena surmised that it must be the hotel portion of the C.P.R. Dining Room. They turned and walked into the first door on their right.

Upon entering Joan's home Serena noticed that it was cosy and warmer than the rest of the building. A hat rack was conveniently located at the entrance. Serena removed her hat and jacket hoping she wasn't making herself too comfortable. It was too warm in the room for a coat. Joan pointed to the table near the window. "Have a seat and I'll get us a cup of coffee."

Serena pulled out a chair and sat at the wooden table, it was a beautifully handmade set of furniture. She took in her surroundings. The floor, too, was smooth wood with a large braided rag rug on the floor between the door and table. A smaller rug was at the doorway. The burgundy window coverings looked like they had been hand sewn of heavy cotton. The walls and ceiling were covered in pine boards. One small sepia toned photo hung on the wall along with a hand-made bundle of things tied with sage and horse hair. She wondered if this was for aromatic purposes.

Joan came back into the room carrying two steaming mugs of coffee. "I took the liberty of adding cream to your coffee, that's how I like mine. I hope that's okay with you." She said setting the mugs on the table. She pulled out a chair, tucked the skirt of her dress beneath her as she took a seat.

Serena's brain clicked into gear and she remembered where she had seen this woman. "Thank you, Joan. Before we get into talking about me and where I came from, I just want to know if you're Joan Hillitser."

Joan's brown eyes got wide and her mouth opened. An eternity seemed to slip by before she answered. "I haven't heard that name in a long time but yes, I'm Joan Hillitser."

THREE
Joan's Story

*Would you tell me, please, which way
I ought to go from here?*
~ Lewis Carroll

"It's a pleasure to meet you, Joan, my name's Serena Tattum." Holding out her hand to introduce herself she continued, "I come from 2012."

A slow smile spread across Joan's face as she reached out to shake Serena's hand. "It's a pleasure to meet you, Serena. You and I have a lot to talk about. We only have half hour before I have to prepare supper for the dining room customers. Ten regulars come in every Friday night."

Both women noted each other's firm handshake and instantly took a liking to one another. Joan let go of her hand and the smile faded.

Joan began, "I know I have a million questions to ask you but I think I better start by telling you about how I got here first."

Serena smiled at Joan knowing she would be okay for the time being and that Rim-Fyre was fed. She listened intently. This was going to be some story.

"Perhaps you already know because you knew my name, that I disappeared on September 21st, 1987, exactly 6 years ago today."

Serena nodded while she sipped on the coffee. It was hot and very good.

"I was 27 years old, still living on the family farm with my parents, helping out with the ranch. Our ranch was just northwest of town here. The day that I disappeared I was out riding fence lines checking for any breaks in the wire before winter. I could have taken a truck or a quad but it was only eight miles of fence to check. It was a beautiful day. Denali, that's my paint gelding, needed to be ridden anyway. He was always such an awesome horse, my best friend, really. He didn't mind that I put on my saddlebags loaded up with a few fencing tools and lunch to go out for a couple hours' ride." Joan paused to have a sip of her coffee.

Serena could only guess that Joan had been unable to tell anyone about her experience. She said nothing but nodded at the appropriate times as Joan went on telling her story.

"I rode the fence line for an hour, stopped and ate lunch while Denali grazed. There were only a few loose wires that required staples but other than that, the day was going great. We continued along the fence line when we scared up several jackrabbits. I don't know where they came from but there must have been a half dozen of them and they exploded right underneath my horse! Poor Denali must have thought he was on fire! While the jackrabbits went every which direction, Denali bucked straight up and ran like hell out into the pasture. I was so surprised, all I could do was hang-on for dear life!" Joan was expressive in the telling of her story. "To make matters worse, the tools in the saddlebags were banging on poor Denali as he was running. It was going to take a mile or so to stop him. So there I was, riding a runaway, hell bent for leather across the pasture as far from those jackrabbits as we could get!"

This prompted another sip of coffee for both of them. Serena didn't take her eyes off Joan, she liked her already. She could just imagine the whole scene unfolding, she smiled at Joan. It was kind of funny but not really because she had a good idea of what was about to happen.

Joan continued, "After the initial terrified sprint, Denali seemed to slow a bit and I took this as a sign to slow him a little more. We were still loping and about three quarters of a mile off of the fence line by now. Denali slowed and got into a smooth relaxed lope, then for no reason he jumped and a blinding flash was all around us. He stopped and stood there shaking. I felt a little shaky too and didn't know why. I took stock of my saddle bags and still had all my stuff. Denali seemed worried all of a sudden and then I took a real good look around me. Something had changed." Both women sipped their coffee which was now half gone.

"Come with me, we'll get the rest of supper prepared and visit more while we're working." Joan went into another room and came out with her sleeping baby in a basket. "Just in case she wakes up," she said smiling.

Serena downed the last of her coffee and followed Joan out the door. They went back down the stairs and to the right which led into a large warm kitchen that smelled of roast beef. A large butcher's block was centralized in the room and on the far wall of the room was the cast iron cook stove. The room was bathed in natural light from two windows, one on the south wall and one to the north. No light fixtures hung from the board ceiling.

Joan set her baby's basket down beside the wood box near the stove. She picked up a pot holder and used it to pick up a metal handle to lift one of the round covers off the top of the stove. She peered in for a look at the wood coals. Wow! Serena was in the dark ages.

Joan replaced the cover and still using the pot holder, opened the side door of the stove and put two more logs in. When the logs ignited from the hot coals, Joan closed the door.

Joan took three large pots down from a rack hung above the stove and set them on the butcher's block. To the right of the stove a counter went all the way to the far north wall. White cotton curtains hung from a wire covered the underside of the counter. Joan pulled back the curtain to reveal baskets filled with potatoes, carrots and beets. On the north wall, a makeshift sink was set up with a drain that went into a bucket. She took enough beets to fill one pot, poured water from a metal bucket underneath the counter and set it on the stove. Joan grabbed two knives from the block on the counter and handed one to Serena.

They each reached for a potato from the basket and began peeling. Joan resumed her story, "It took me a while to realize what changed after Denali and I came back in time. First thing I noticed was the rocks on the ground around us, they were in a circle, with another circle around it and an entry path or something on the outer circle. The rocks were put there on purpose and we were standing right in the middle. There were no power poles or fence lines in the distance, the hills were different too. We stayed there for a little while but I knew the general direction of home and of course Denali did, too. When we got to where the farm should have been there was no sign of home. We stood there for some time and Denali let out the most pitiful neigh I ever heard. I knew something was horribly wrong and I got scared and started to cry."

A splash of water was added to the potatoes they peeled and set on the stove, too. The women peeled and prepared carrots while Joan continued with her story.

"It was about eight miles into Swift Current for us from our farm. I figured that was my best shot at finding someone. Denali and I took it fairly slow. He was already sweaty from his run with the rabbit scare, so we walked most of the way."

Using the pot holders, Joan removed the large roasting pan of meat from the oven and set it on the butcher's block. She pointed over to the floor by the sink where Serena was standing, "See that handle on the floor? Pull it up."

Serena leaned down to pull on the leather handle nailed to the floor, noticing that there was a large square cut around it that blended in with the boards. There was little resistance when she pulled on the handle as a large box came up out of the floor. Serena felt the cold air come up with the box where the front side was open. It was a fridge! Well, not a fridge like Serena knew a fridge but it served the purpose.

"Would you get the two pies out of there for me?"

She let go of the handle and surprisingly the box stayed in place. Two pies and other items were on the shelves in the box. Serena removed the pies from the box and set them on the butcher's block. Joan put them in the oven to cook while they served supper.

"What is this thing?"

"Oh that! It's a dumbwaiter." Joan chuckled as she put the second pie in the oven.

She thought *a dumb what?* But then thought better of the remark and refrained from saying it. "How do you close it?"

"Just push down on the top, it's operated by a pulley. We have about ten minutes to sit down before I set up for supper."

The women sat down on the chairs up against the stair wall, Joan sighed heavily.

"How old is your baby?" Serena asked.

"Katie is nearly six months old now." She said proudly. "I love her dearly."

"I love my kids too. I really miss them." Serena said sadly.

Joan's arm went around her shoulder, "I'm so sorry for you and your family. I'm going to see what I can do to help you but as you can see I have chores to do first."

"So what name are you using while you are here? Everyone will assume because you have short hair and dress the way that you do that you're a man; one that can't grow facial hair worth two-hoots." Joan laughed at that. "Sorry, just trying to get our story straight here before my husband gets home so I can introduce you."

Serena smiled at her humour. "I was using my husband's name, Derek."

"Alright then Derek, you are my cousin from down east on my mom's side of the family, that way you can use your own last name, which is what again?"

"Tattum."

"You rode the train with your horse to Moose Jaw thinking that's where you were supposed to find me, only to find out you had to ride three days to Swift Current. Help me out here with your story." Joan prompted.

"I fell off my horse, got knocked out, and when I came to, my provisions were gone but my horse never left me. Then I found my way here by asking folks I came in contact with. Well at least that part is true." Serena added.

Joan smiled, "Perfect, you look like you would be about thirty, a young thirty year old man around these parts anyway. You'll fit right in. So, you are my cousin, of course I haven't seen you for more than six years and we have family news to catch up on. I think Mac will be okay with that story and we have a room just down the hall for you to stay in."

Joan got up from the chair and removed plates from the shelving above the counter. "I'll let you cut the roast and dish up portions while I take coffee out to the customers who will be coming in the door soon." Joan handed her the pot holders, a three pronged fork and a large butcher knife as she took a tray full of cups out to the dining room.

In a whirl of preparations, Serena cut the roast into portions, drained the potatoes, carrots and beets. She poured a little cool water from the bucket over the beets to cool them to peel without burning her hands. Meanwhile, Joan was greeting her regular customers and served them coffee or tea. She returned to the kitchen to show Serena how much food to place on each plate, nine servings were prepared. Joan took out three plates at a time while Serena set out the portions. Once all of the customers in the dining room were served their meals they put the rest of the food into a pot and placed it on the warm stove. The pie was baked and removed from the oven then it, too, was portioned and served to the customers. A kettle of water was heating on the stove for washing up. Serena found a plug for the makeshift sink and began washing dishes and placed them on a cotton cloth laid out on the counter. Joan served more coffee or tea for the mostly male customers in the dining room.

When the customers paid for their meals and were gone, Joan closed the doors and left one lamp lit near the front lobby desk. Serena had plates and excess pots washed already. All that was left to clean were cups and saucers that Joan was bringing into the kitchen.

"Oh wow, thank you so much for your help! We'll be able to eat supper in no time." Joan smiled. "Mac will be so surprised that I'm upstairs before dark." She brought one of the oil lamps from the dining room and set it on the butcher's block. It cast a warm glow in the dimming light.

They worked together in silence for fifteen minutes to finish cleaning up and put dishes away. Joan tossed one more log on the stove to keep the chill off. The temperature was dipping near freezing point and it kept the building toasty warm.

Joan gently scooped up Katie's basket and Serena brought the pot and remaining pie to eat their supper in Joan's suite. The baby's basket was set in the doorway and Joan went to get a lamp lit, along with place settings for three of them while Serena set the food on the table.

Joan's husband walked in right behind them and asked. "Who have we got here, another stray?"

He wasn't a very large man, six feet tall with an average build. His complexion and over-all appearance was that of a man who had been very sick at one point in his life. A shiny bald head was revealed when he took his cap off.

Joan immediately introduced Serena, "Mac, I'd like you to meet my cousin Derek Tattum from out east. Derek, this is my husband Maximilian MacMillan."

Maximilian smiled at Serena with a lopsided grin and held his hand out to shake hers. "Ah now Derek, don't listen to Joanie here, everyone calls me Mac, pleasure to meet someone from Joanie's family. Please do have a seat and we'll have our supper."

Serena shook Mac's hand graciously and they sat down to eat. They bowed their heads while Mac thanked God for the meal. "Amen," they chorused in unison.

Mac filled his plate and Joan split the remainder of the food between Serena and herself. Serena spoke little unless a question was directed specifically her way. Joan and Mac filled each other in on their day's activities. Then Joan explained how Serena got misdirected and ended up finding her way to their door. Serena agreed that she had planned on surprising Joan with a visit and could hardly be expecting him to show up on their doorstep. Mac was just happy to see his Joanie happy. And that finally, after all these years, someone from her family came to visit. Joan and Serena just smiled knowingly at one another.

Serena hadn't realized how hungry she was until she started eating. Even though it wasn't a fancy meal it was delicious. Joan set a piece of pie on everyone's plate which was some sort of orange berry, rather tangy but good just the same; the pie crust was perfect and flaky.

Mac invited Serena down to the barn to feed the horses while Joan cleaned up supper dishes and tended to little Katie who was now wailing that she needed her mama. Serena went with Mac to the barn to check on Rim-Fyre.

The evening air was brisk and cool as they left the Dining Room building and walked to the barn.

"So Derek, what are your plans now that you made it to Swift Current?" Mac asked as they entered the barn. He held the lantern high and located a hook for the lantern while they checked on and fed the horses.

"I suspect I'll be finding myself some employment here soon and earn my own keep," Serena offered. Serena had no plan but didn't want Joan's husband thinking she was going to take something for nothing.

Mac inquired further, "And are you planning on breeding horses with this outstanding stallion you have? I had a look at him when I got home but he wasn't too keen on having me near him." He pointed to the trough and a bucket, "better water him. I couldn't get close enough to him when I came in earlier."

Serena carried a bucket of water over to Rim-Fyre, now nickering softly to her. "I really liked the look of this particular horse from the Quebec country in the east. We seem to have developed a close bond on our journey here. I think he'll make fine breeding stock." Rim-Fyre took a deep drink out of the bucket she offered him. She stroked his neck while he drank and watched his ears flick with every swallow.

"You might make good stud fees off him if you offered him for breeding, his like are very rarely seen in this part of the country. He has good bone and feet under him." Mac stated as he carried hay to the other two horses in the cozy barn. The horses were creating just enough body heat to keep the chill off the air.

"Well, I will keep that in mind Mac, thanks." Serena went to the hay storage area of the barn and pitched another forkful of hay to Rim-Fyre.

With chores done, Mac lifted the lantern from its hook and closed the barn door. They walked to the east side of the Dining Room building where there were two large boxes with hinged lids. A black tin pail was set nearby.

"Here, hold the lantern for me while I get a bucket of coal for the night. It's going to be a cool one. Heavy frost tonight, I can feel it in my bones." Mac lifted the lid and used a short handled shovel that was in there to scoop out enough coal to fill the bucket. As they made their way to the door, they could begin to see their breath in the cool night air.

Joan made tea upon their return, dishes were done and Katie was fast asleep. Serena had no idea what time it was but was beginning to feel the weight of the day. Sleep would soon beckon her, too. The warmth of the room only added to feeling lethargic after being out in the cool evening air.

They sat down at the table for a cup of tea, engaged in small talk and discussed the next day's activities. Mac was working in the morning to prepare for the train's scheduled arrival the following afternoon. He finished his tea and excused himself as he was off to work by five in the morning.

Joan poured another cup of tea. "I still have so much to tell you and then you are going to have to fill me in on how you ended up here. Now where were we?"

Joan went back to her story to tell Serena that there was only a conglomeration of white tents with wood stoves in them when she arrived in Swift Current. At the time, it was still known as Pile of Bones, largely due to the buffalo bones littering the prairies and piled everywhere. There wasn't even a railroad track yet. She had been terrified out of her mind but at the same time, determined to survive. Several men from the Canadian Pacific Railway were camped there surveying for the railroad track that was coming the following year from Moose Jaw. Joan had arrived in 1881. Mac had been Joan's savior because he was deathly ill with influenza. His workmates didn't want to take care of him for fear of illness and they had to finish surveying west of the camp. Mac was on death's doorstep when Joan rode into camp. He was one of the top surveyors and the crew couldn't spare someone to look after him. They didn't care where she came from so Joan was hired on the spot. In exchange for her room and board, she was required to cook their meals and care for Mac, hopefully bringing him back from the dead.

She went on to explain to Serena that the days flew by. Mac was really sick and the influenza had him in its grip. Joan was grateful to have a cot to sleep on and heat from a wood stove even though the wood had to be retrieved from deadfall near the creek and water had to be hauled from there, too. It was weeks before Mac began to make any real progress in getting well but with Joan's care he made a comeback. His lungs were damaged from the influenza and he was weak for a long time. It was November before he was strong enough to walk a short distance.

Fall turned to winter and a brutal winter it was. It was so bad in fact that sometimes the Indians camping there would leave logs near their tent flap so that Joan wouldn't have to go out and gather wood in the worst of storms. They nearly froze to death that winter in the tents. There had been very little time to mourn the loss of her old life in order to merely survive in this one.

Provisions were brought late in December before the worst storms hit in January. By spring, Mac had regained most of his strength. Mac and Joan made the trek to Moose Jaw in early April to see where the track building crew was at and how long it would take them to reach Pile of Bones. A native scout accompanied them on their journey.

They met up with the track building crew on the third day riding east of Pile of Bones and rode for the rest of the day to get to Moose Jaw. Joan hadn't realized how far 95 miles was on horseback.

She had been with Mac here for six months. They fell in love with one another out of necessity; him for his health, and her for any other connection to the real world from which she had been separated. Perhaps she was needed here more than in her old life in 1987. Mac asked Joan to marry him and she did on April 17th, 1882, in Moose Jaw.

While in Moose Jaw, Mac was offered the position of manager of the new C.P.R. Dining Room that would be constructed in what was going to become Swift Current. They wanted to have it running by the time the first train was scheduled to pull into the train stop at the end of 1882. Mac was more than happy to accept the position. They then returned to Swift Current a newly married couple.

That was where Joan's story would have to end for the night, "Sorry, we have to get up early and make breakfast for the customers staying here this evening and it's getting late." Joan apologized.

"It's alright Joan, I'm tired too." Serena smiled wearily. "I'm just wondering something though. It's 1887 now, right?"

Joan nodded.

"So that means you've been here for six years." She nodded again and looked questioningly at Serena. "But when I travelled back in time today, was that just today?" She shook her head, "it was 2012, so in my time you've been missing for twenty-five years. Do you have an idea why that might be?"

Joan looked perplexed for a moment, "No, I don't. That's quite a discrepancy isn't it? I'll leave you with that thought and take you to your room."

Joan handed Serena another lantern, directed her down the hall to another room and opened the door for her. "I'll knock on your door in the morning. Good night Serena." And with that she turned and left.

Serena entered the room and closed the door setting the lamp on the small night table by the bed. The single bed frame held a thin mattress with several quilts stacked up at the foot end and a yellowed pillow case covered the only pillow. It wasn't anything fancy but it was a warm place to lay her head for the night. She felt as though every ounce of energy was suddenly drained from her body and couldn't remember ever being this tired in all her life. Not even when Jess and Cole were babies and all those nights of no sleep.

That thought brought tears that silently coursed down her cheeks. *Would she ever see her kids and husband again?* She removed her outer layer of clothing, spread the quilts out on the bed, crawled under the covers and fell into an exhausted sleep.

Derek lay in bed alone, tired but unable to sleep. He played out the last six hours, ever since Cole had called him at work in a panic because mom wasn't home and something was wrong. Serena's mom had come to the house to stay with Jess and Cole until he got home to discover that indeed something was wrong. Serena and their stallion Rim-Fyre were missing. She hadn't taken her purse or any ID with her, no keys, no note to say she was going anywhere. It was unlike Serena in every way imaginable.

Derek, Serena's dad and brother had driven every mile of grid roads for a twenty mile radius of the farm until it was too dark to see. There was no sign of a horse and rider anywhere. They had stopped at every farm house in the area to ask if anyone had seen her which turned up nothing. When they returned to the house Jess wasn't visibly upset but Cole had run to him in tears crying for his mom. "Oh dad, where could she be? Is she dead?" he asked. It took hours to calm him enough to get him to bed. They decided they would go out on quads and horseback in the morning to search one more time before they called the police to report Serena missing.

Serena wasn't dead. If she was, he would feel it in his heart and right now his heart and mind could still feel her. She was far away, just not dead. "My darling Serena, if you can hear me, hang in there sweetheart. I'll find you and bring you home, I promise." He felt the words had to be said out loud.

From the moment he'd seen Serena the summer after her graduation, he'd been head over in heels in love with her. She was his girl, his woman, companion and best friend. He knew that over the years he'd slacked off some in letting her know how much she really meant to him. Serena loved to dance and they always seemed closer when they went out and had fun together. Work and the kids were taking a toll on their marriage. He swore he'd change that once Serena was home safely in his arms.

With his eyes closed against the darkness, Derek whispered softly, "I love you sweet Serena, more than you know." And with that he slipped off into a dream.

FOUR

Dreaming

*That which dreamed can never be lost,
can never be undreamed.*
~ Neil Gaiman

Her cell phone rang as Serena forked the last of the hay over the fence. With phone in hand she checked the time and number. It was after 6 PM and it was Derek calling to tell her he was going to be late again. She was pissed.

"Hello?"

"Hey Hon, I'm going to be late. I'm having a beer with the guys. Go ahead and eat supper with the kids, I'll be home in half hour."

"Fine, I'll see you when you get home."

She heard him say "I love you," as she clicked the phone shut and shoved it back in her pocket.

The pitchfork hit the hay bale with more force than was necessary and it stuck in to the hilt. Serena knew she needed to diffuse her anger before going to the house to share supper with the kids. *Why can't he just come home and have supper with us? See and talk to the kids, then go out for a drink after.* It pissed her off that she was always the one being the responsible adult in the house and making sure that the needs of their children were met. *What about the father's responsibility? He should be interacting with his kids and spending quality time with them too. What about her?*

Serena shifted her focus to her horses. The three mares she purchased the year before looked amazing. Their coats shone in the early evening sun, already showing signs of thickening in preparation for the long winter ahead. Specifically chosen for their conformation and bloodlines, these mares would carry the future of their Canadian horse herd. Tess stood the tallest at 15.3 HH, her overall appearance was pretty, tall and refined with substantial bone and large hard hooves for which Canadians were known. Nadia was shorter and wider in stature, longer in the neck and back with a notably pretty head and wide set eyes. Nadia's mane and tail were abundant and extremely long. Both mares were black as coal. Majestic stood out with her blood bay body coloring and flowing black mane and tail. Majestic lived up to her name and made her an irresistible purchase for Serena. The mare looked very much like a female version of a painting Serena had seen of Justin Morgan. In this particular horse it was easy to see how the Canadian horse influenced the Morgan breed so many years ago. All her beautiful attributes combined with powerful limbs and hard wide feet made her an exemplary Canadian mare. Serena was proud of her little band of mares that she chose to pair with her foundation bred stallion, Rim-Fyre.

The two geldings were looking at her from the other gate in the corrals, waiting for her to make her way over and give them attention, too. Serena turned to see the two large but beautiful heads over the gate eagerly awaiting her approach, one black as night and the other as red as a mahogany door. "How are my boys tonight?" She asked as she walked towards the geldings. A soft 'her-her-her' came from her bay roan, Pepper. This greeting made her smile as she approached the geldings. She put her cheek on Pepper's face and he leaned right into her as she hugged his large head. Slade waited for his turn to get a rubbing under his jaw just the way he liked, then she ran both her hands gently over his brows and down the side of his face to his muzzle where she planted a big kiss. "I love you guys, you're so sweet and you're always here to give me comfort when I need it. Night, guys." She gave them each another kiss on the muzzle and turned to go back to the house. She had her horse-fix now and hoped she was calm enough to deal with her inebriated husband when he got home.

She hadn't realized she spent nearly an hour out at the barn, it was now dark and would be she would be in a hurry to get the kids fed and ready for bed. As she approached the door to the house, Serena could hear Jess and Cole screaming at each other. She was really hoping for a more relaxed meal time than this.

"If you don't give me back my shark tooth right now, I'm going to throw this rock at you!" nine year old Cole shouted at his sister.

Serena walked in the door to see that her sixteen year old daughter had Cole by the throat. If she thought she was pissed off at her husband before, she was fuming now.

"JESS!" Serena barked slamming the door for emphasis. "I told you before that violence was no way to solve anything, and that beating on your little brother was equivalent to me beating him which would be considered child abuse. Now go to your room, I'll deal with you later!"

Jess ran past her mom and went downstairs to the temporary safety of her room.

Serena exhaled in exhaustion as she took off her barn coat and hung it on the horseshoe rack on the wall. She felt deflated as she stepped up from the porch into the kitchen.

Cole ran over and hugged her fiercely, "I'm sorry, Mom. She wouldn't give me my shark tooth necklace. I think she hates me."

Serena hugged her son back and held him to her chest for as long as he would let her. "She doesn't hate you, Cole, but her emotions are right there at the surface and you know exactly how to get her mad. We better have something to eat."

They sat down to the meal of lasagna, bowed their heads to give thanks and ate in amicable silence. Cole wasn't his usual exuberant self.

"How come you and Jess didn't come out and help me chore?" she directed at her son.

"Sorry, Mom, I was busy playing and Jess did her homework, right up 'til just before you came in. Then she got all mean and took my necklace out of the bathroom and was buggin' me about it. And then I got mad and she got mad. And then you came in and got mad, too." He glanced up at his mom to see what kind of reaction that last sentence might provoke.

She felt ashamed for being so angry and wearily answered him, "I'm sorry, too, for getting so mad, I'll go talk to Jess. Dad won't be home until later."

"Oh, should I phone him and see when he's coming home?"

"No, go have a shower and get ready for bed. I'll go talk to Jess."

Serena walked downstairs into the basement and gently knocked on Jess's door. "Can I come in?" she asked slowly opening the door.

Jess was lying in bed reading with her back to the door. "You can come in."

Serena went in and sat on the edge of the bed.

Jess rolled over and sat up. "I'm sorry, Mom, he just knows how to get me so mad. I know you told me to walk away when I get mad but he was slapping and kicking at me before I had a chance to leave."

Serena turned to hug her daughter. "Try not to aggravate the situation. Make up with Cole and remember to protect him instead of making a mortal enemy out of your little brother. Please."

"I'll try, Mom. I just should have come out to the barn to help you chore and play with the fillies. That always makes me feel better." She said hugging her mom extra hard before she let go.

Serena got up from the bed, "Come up and have something to eat. There's lots of lasagna left."

After supper Serena played a game of go-fish with Cole, while Jess went back to her room to read. It was already half past nine when Serena tucked her son into bed. They said bedtime prayers together then she kissed his forehead and went to say good night to Jess.

She sat down at the table with a hot cup of tea when the lights from Derek's truck shone into the yard. Serena felt the anxious rolling of her stomach, a feeling she hated every time her husband had too much to drink. Not every time, but many times when he'd been drinking that's when they would fight and she hated it. She hoped tonight wouldn't turn out to be a fight night.

She located the local paper she picked up earlier today and stuck her nose in it just as Derek came through the door.

"Smells good in here, what's for supper?" Derek asked removing his work boots and jacket in the porch.

"Lasagna," she stated.

"Well you won't believe who I ran into at the bar," he continued.

No, you're right I wouldn't, she thought to herself. He went on to tell her all about some old friend he met that he hadn't seen in ten years or so and all of the B.S. that went with the conversation. She wasn't really paying any attention to whoever he was talking about or what had transpired during the conversation. Serena tuned it out and his voice took on the hum of a drone of bees.

Derek helped himself to a plate of half warm lasagna and placed it in the microwave to heat while he rummaged in the fridge to find some juice or milk to have with his meal. There was no beer in there so she knew he was done drinking for the day. The microwave beeped. Derek grabbed his plate and went straight into the living room to sit in his favorite chair, watch TV and eat his supper.

Serena felt better with no retaliation from Derek so focused on the newspaper she had in front of her. She opened it to the second and third pages and her eyes were instantly drawn to a photo of a young woman on a Paint horse. The photo was in black and white but she could see that the horse was a bay overo with minimal white patches and four high white stockings. She read the inscription below the photo. 'Photo of Joan Hillitser on her Paint gelding Denali, in 1987 before their disappearance'. *1987? Disappearance? What? How had she missed that? Oh right, she would have been in grade 8.* The heading on the article read, **Missing 25 Years. What happened to Joan Hillitser?** She continued reading. The article went on to tell the story of this young twenty-seven year old woman and her horse, Denali, and how they went missing on September 21st of 1987. Joan went out for a ride that afternoon and never returned. A search by local police, friends and family was conducted and lasted more than a week with no sign of young Joan and her horse. *This was the prairies for Pete's sake, where could she have gone?* They had even gone so far as to hire a tracker with little or no luck. She had gone riding in their cattle pasture that covered more than a half section of land, either cattle or other horse tracks had marred their path and it was never discovered where she had ridden exactly. It was as if the ground itself had swallowed her up with no trace. Now twenty-five years later, her family had received permission from the city and the Rural Municipality to erect a plaque in honor of their daughter at the historical site in the city known as The Battleford Trail. Their farm also had a small remnant of the old Battleford Trail and they didn't want citizens of the city and surrounding area to forget their daughter. In all those years they had never come anywhere close to figuring out what had happened to Joan. No one seemed to know anything. *'Weird.'*

"Hey, Honey, do you ever remember hearing anything about this woman and her horse that went missing twenty-five years ago?" Serena directed at her husband in the living room.

There was no reply. She got up from her place at the table and walked around the corner into the living room to find Derek fast asleep in his chair, the empty plate in his lap. She went over, gently picked the plate up from his lap and carried it into the kitchen. A combination of a couple beers and a hot meal after a long hard day at work proved to be a tonic for sleep for him.

After a quick shower, she towel dried her hair, put a t-shirt, underwear and lounge pants on and turned off all the lights and TV in the house. It felt good to crawl into bed between microfiber sheets, snuggle in and close her eyes. Life was pretty good. She knew Derek would be up and gone in the morning by the time she woke up to get the kids ready for school. "Good-night, Honey, I love you." she whispered to the dark wishing it was different though as she drifted off to sleep.

Serena jerked awake with the knock on the door.

"Good morning! Breakfast will be ready in ten minutes."

A quick glance around the unfamiliar room and the feel of the heavy cotton fabric against her skin reminded Serena where and when she was. *A dream, it was just a dream. Why couldn't 1887 be a dream instead? What she wouldn't give to go back and do things differently. Everything was left in such a mess with Derek, now more than ever she vowed to get home to let him know how much he meant to her.* She laid her head back on the pillow with her eyes open to take that in for a minute. She wanted to bawl but that wasn't going to solve anything. *What would today bring?*

How was she going to get back home?

FIVE

A Plan

High expectations are the key to everything
~ Sam Walton

Enough light filtered in through the window for Serena to see the outline of the walls and sparse furnishings. She quickly dressed and walked down the stairs, it was eerily quiet in the building this early in the morning.

Joan greeted Serena with a "Good Morning!" and a smile as she rounded the corner from the stairway into the warm kitchen. She graciously poured a mug of coffee and put a healthy dollop of cream in it from the quart sealer on the counter.

After a sip of the fresh boiled coffee Serena smiled, "Morning to you, too. It was a short night."

"I can understand that," Joan acknowledged. "It's going to feel like a long day today."

Serena sipped her coffee while Joan got breakfast ingredients out of the dumbwaiter. Soon skillets filled with sizzling bacon, eggs and potatoes releasing delicious aroma throughout the room. Serena's stomach growled in anticipation as she finished the first half cup of coffee. The bell at the dining room entrance was ringing and breakfast customers were filtering in. Footsteps of the upstairs guests coming down the staircase for their breakfast sent Joan to greet them with coffee pot in hand. Serena prepared the plates with food and was surprised that toast could be made in an oven.

An hour later they were upstairs eating their breakfast. Katie was cooing in her basket. Mac had already gone to work this morning and would be back for lunch. The other horses were fed earlier this morning when Mac left. Serena would go feed Rim-Fyre herself. Joan assured her she would look after breakfast clean up and take care of Katie while she went to the barn.

The brilliant sun was beginning to crest the eastern horizon. Frost clung to the grass and buildings. Serena breathed in the sun warmed air as she made her way to the barn. A waft of horse smell assailed her as she opened the barn door, and a gentle her-her-her greeting came from Rim-Fyre. "Morning, Rim. How's my guy this morning? Hungry and thirsty I bet." She filled the bucket from the barrel and brought it to him. Rim-Fyre nuzzled her jacket front and dipped his nose in the bucket for a deep drink of water. Once he drank his fill, she brought him hay which he dove into with gusto. Serena found a brush stuck in the crook of the posts that held the beams in the barn and she brushed him while he ate.

"I don't know what the plan is for today Rim, but I sure hope Joan has some idea how to help us get home.

You want to go home, too, don't you?" Rim-Fyre stopped chewing for a moment and turned to nuzzle her hand gently. He resumed eating his hay while Serena hugged his thick neck and breathed in his horse scent. He gave her comfort in this place of uncertainty. "I'm going to go talk to Joan, I'll be back later. Enjoy your breakfast," she added, giving him a final squeeze on his neck before she walked out the door into the fresh crisp morning air.

The hot dark liquid splashed into the cup. "One more coffee while I tell you the rest of my story, then we best get lunch prepared. My friend Helena said she would watch Katie while we go out for a few hours this afternoon. There's someone important I want you to meet." Joan sat down at the table across from Serena.

After Joan married Mac, they returned to Swift Current. Not only did Mac have to oversee the building of the new C.P.R. Dining Room and Round House but he also had to go out several times to assist with surveying in the west for the new railway that was coming. That spring and summer they lived in the same tent they had occupied during the previous winter. Joan had much to learn about living in this time because it didn't offer the comforts of her previous home.

While Mac was working, she would ride Denali south along the banks of the creek, searching out a better fishing spot and exploring the surroundings. On one such ride, she came across several tipis set up on a knoll near the creek. Denali seemed eager to explore further. There were a handful of women and children near the water's edge who scattered as soon as they saw her. Joan was remorseful that they would run from her but Denali insisted on charging into the fray and introducing himself. One Indian man came forward with confidence at their approach. Denali stopped at a respectable distance for conversation.

Joan felt out of her element but she offered a "Hi, I'm Joan MacMillan. I come from the camp over there." She pointed the direction she had come from.

The man stepped forward looking angry as he pointed Joan back the way she came. "You go back now!" he told her firmly.

Joan was embarrassed. She didn't expect to be sent away. She tried in vain to turn Denali back to camp but he refused to budge which only added to her embarrassment. He even went so far as to take a step toward the Indian man as if to defy his decision to send them away. Joan tried once again to turn Denali away from the Indian camp to no avail and resorted to dismounting which was even more humiliating to the point where she was nearly in tears.

Laughter erupted from the Indian who had sent her away. He surprised her when he spoke, "Your horse insists we speak words, maybe he is wiser than us all. You are a long way from home, Miss Joan. I am known as Nawat Sinopa. Please come sit and we will talk."

Joan scowled at Denali but followed this man to sit on the ground at a low fire in front of a tipi. Denali seemed pleased and stood calmly behind Joan as she sat and spoke with Nawat Sinopa.

Her conversation with the Indian man that first day was a short one. She found out that he had learned to speak English several years before and in the past scouted for traders and surveyors when they'd come out to explore this land. He also worked with the North West Mounted Police or N.W.M.P. for a time. Nawat Sinopa was very spiritual and had a sense about him of things that were not of this world. That day he introduced her to the people of their small village so that she would feel welcome if she came to visit again. They loaded her saddlebags with dried meat and berries and invited her to return.

Serena took a drink of her cooling coffee, "Did he say why he sent you away?"

"No, not really, maybe he was afraid or because he could sense something about where I came from," Joan surmised.

Denali and Joan went back to visit the little village as often as they could, each time she learned more about Nawat Sinopa. His great uncle was a Medicine Man and lived up on the great bench to the southwest of Swift Current. It was from his great uncle that he had heard grand stories of sudden appearances of Spirits, animal or human, many moons ago when his uncle was a young brave singing in the buffalo. He told of the Great Stone Circles and how some of them possessed Great Magic. Nawat Sinopa did not know how the Great Magic from the Creator worked but he was sure that his uncle would know more. Sadly for Joan, she would not get the chance to find out. Mac refused to give his consent for her to leave for days to go to the bench exploring. She could not tell him why she wanted to go. In her own way, this was her admission of love for Mac and maybe she was meant to stay here in this alternate time. Nawat Sinopa had helped her spiritually deal with this decision.

That fall, Mac and Joan moved into the most modern facilities of the time in Swift Current. They were now the proud caretakers of the C.P.R. Dining Room. It would remain their home as long as Mac was the manager. Nawat Sinopa's village moved further south for the winter, she didn't see him again until the following spring.

"I had a baby boy on October 17th, 1884. He was stillborn. We named him Joshua Michael and buried him the next day. It was the saddest time of our lives," Joan concluded as a tear slipped from her eye. "We better get dinner ready."

Serena was instantly heartbroken for Joan over that sad admission but the abrupt change of subject meant it wasn't open for discussion. This was such a harsh existence. She gave her a brief hug before they left the suite and went down to the kitchen to prepare dinner for paying guests and themselves.

Baby Katie assumed her assigned place near the warm stove in her basket. She had been such a good baby sleeping the whole time Joan and Serena talked.

"Joan, won't Mac think it's strange me helping you in the kitchen and all? Seeing as I'm your male cousin?"

Serena was surprised at Joan's outburst of laughter. "Heaven's no! Every chance I get, I put him to work in the kitchen, too! He's probably so thankful it's you and not him."

This revelation made Serena laugh, too, and put her at ease. "So what's the plan for this afternoon?" she inquired.

"Helena is going to watch Katie, after I feed and change her of course. Then you and I are going to go meet Nawat Sinopa and see if we can't get you out to meet this uncle of his and perhaps find some answers to get you back home. You can tell me your story on the way."

Rim-Fyre and Denali were saddled and ready to go. Rim-Fyre stood and waited patiently for Serena to bridle him and check the saddle again before being led outside. Once in the sunlight it took a few minutes for everyone's eyes to adjust from the dim light of the barn. Serena and Joan mounted their horses.

"Lead the way," Serena indicated to Joan. They immediately turned the horses south and crossed the two sets of railway tracks. There were several plain tipis to the southeast of the tracks where the Métis camped out.

The landscape seemed rather sparsely populated in comparison to what Serena was used to. She'd only been here 28 hours. It felt like an eternity because this wasn't really where she wanted to be.

"It's nearly two miles to the Indian Camp south of here. Which direction did you say you came from?" Joan asked.

"From the south, perhaps just a little further than where we are heading right now," Serena went on with her story. "Night before last, I had an awful evening. I was mad at the world because things weren't going the way that I thought they should. Derek was out drinking with his buddies and I was at home with the kids again, feeding them supper, dealing with all the day to day parental duties without my spouse to share it with me. Then Jess and Cole were fighting yet too, it was all too much."

"How old are your kids?"

"Jess is sixteen going on twenty and Cole is nine." A comfortable silence passed while both women were thinking.

Serena was in awe at Rim-Fyre's behaviour, ignoring Joan's gelding, Denali. He was walking calmly even though she knew he must want to run and stretch out his limbs. Rim was different here, way different, he was acting more like a gelding.

Serena continued, "Yesterday morning after I got the kids on the bus to school, I decided that taking Rim here out for a ride was probably the best thing to do to relax, de-stress and figure out what was truly important. I hadn't ridden Rim for a few weeks so I knew he needed to get out, too. We went out along the creek bank on the other side of the creek like I always do and on our way back, Rim jumped over some stones and there was a blinding flash of light. I think that's when it happened because after that he was vibrating and I felt disoriented."

"Sounds very similar to what happened to me," Joan added. "Did you notice anything about the rocks?"

"There was nothing really notable about them before the flash of light. The past few years we had lots of rain, so the prairie grass was longer than I'd ever remembered seeing it. The rocks were helter-skelter and only a handful of them were visible above the grass. After Rim tripped, I tried to memorize the formation of the rocks, they were far more visible. They appeared to be in a large circle and there was an opening in the circle facing the south with a path. It's only a few miles, I can take you there one day and show you if you have time."

"Sure, maybe we'll do that. Let's lope to the top of the rise there by the cut banks." And with that, Joan let Denali have his head and loped off ahead.

Rim-Fyre was waiting for this, without any prompting from Serena he was beside Denali stride for stride all the way to the top of the hill. The horses slowed to a walk of their own accord once they'd reached the crest of the hill and could see across the open valley below. In the distance near the creek, they could make out the tipis of the little Indian village from this vantage point. *Funny I didn't notice them yesterday when I rode by here,* Serena thought. They continued down the hill toward the creek, a narrow trail through the grass led the way.

"I should tell you more about Nawat Sinopa before we get there." Joan paused. "He's very, how do you say? Charismatic and handsome, perhaps not something you would expect from Indians of this time. In some ways he seems sly and cunning too. Even after these years of speaking with him, I'm still not exactly sure how trustworthy he is. It might just be me, too. He was named appropriately. Sinopa means fox in their language. Perhaps he is somewhat fox-like."

"What does the first part of his name mean?" Serena inquired. "Nawat? It sounds funny like now what? I hope I can say it without laughing."

Joan turned serious. "You can't laugh at his name. It would be most disrespectful, he could send us away and refuse to help you."

Serena showed remorse at her remark and hung her head. "Sorry, I meant no disrespect."

"It's ok," Joan encouraged. "Nawat means left handed. I think once you meet him, you will think differently. He has a great presence about him, very much like your Rim-Fyre who looks like he's really trying to repress what he could be. Or is he always like that? I'm guessing not simply because Denali was different when we first arrived at this alternate time, too."

"Wow! Are you really that observant?" Serena looked down at Rim.

"Serena I've been here for six years already. The first two years I noticed everything and hoped upon hope that I might find the way back home. My love for Mac kept me here. I hope you can understand that. Maybe if Mac had allowed me to meet Nawat Sinopa's uncle things would have turned out differently," Joan paused, "but he didn't and I felt that I owed it to him to obey his wishes. Or... perhaps I needed to be here for you."

With that said they rode into the little Indian village and were warmly greeted by a few of the tribeswomen and of course, Nawat Sinopa.

"Greetings, Joan!" Came from the Indian brave Serena could only assume was Nawat Sinopa. His long black hair only added to his masculine good looks. Serena tried not to stare, instead looking to Joan for an introduction and some help here. She was very much aware of the fact that she was married to Derek and had children but she wasn't dead either, this guy would be considered eye candy in her time.

"Hello, my friend," Joan replied in greeting dismounting from Denali.

Serena wondered how Joan did it, mount and dismount with all those skirts wrapped around her legs like that without getting tangled up or hooked on the saddle anywhere. She took that as a sign to dismount Rim-Fyre, too, so she stepped down with grace and walked closer to Joan and Denali. Rim was subdued.

"Who have you brought with you this fine day?" Nawat Sinopa indicated towards Serena. "Are we having a big pow-wow today?" he asked in jest. "Or have you come to make trade?"

Joan smiled brilliantly, "It's a pow-wow of sorts, Nawat Sinopa. This is my new friend, Serena."

Serena tried not to let her mouth gape at Joan's admission of her real name, which indicated she was female. She was most certainly dressed the same as any man in this time.

The impressive man cocked one eyebrow in Serena's direction. "Come sit at my fire and tell me about it." He then pointed at the women and said something in his native tongue that indicated that they should busy themselves with something. Several of the older men had come to stand close by so he turned and spoke with them as well. They went back to their previous tasks or sitting outside their tipis. He turned and indicated to the women to join him.

Denali and Rim-Fyre took their respective places standing behind Joan and Serena as they sat down facing Nawat Sinopa across his fire. He eyed Serena questioningly as she tried to hide her identity under her hat and beneath her large overcoat.

"Greetings, Serena." Nawat Sinopa allowed her name to run over his tongue like a bittersweet candy. Then he directed the conversation to a more familiar face, "Joan tell me, what is this? How is this woman that is dressed like a man your friend?"

"Nawat Sinopa, my friend. Do you remember when I first came here and I told you about the magic stones that brought me here from a far off time?" Joan asked with sincerity inflected in her voice.

He nodded.

"Serena here, too, has come from a far off time through the magic stones, only even further than from where I came. Where she comes from it is acceptable for women to dress and even work like men. To her knowledge she was brought here not of her making, she has a family where she came from and that family needs to be together. Can you take her to meet your uncle to see if he can help her?"

"Joan, my uncle is a very old man. I have not seen him in some time, I do not even know if he yet lives. What if he cannot help with such things?"

"I'm willing to take that chance," Serena spoke and Rim-Fyre let out a long snort for emphasis.

Nawat Sinopa did not direct his gaze at Serena but looked long at Rim-Fyre, the horse peered uncomfortably into his soul until he looked away. "Wait here, I must speak with the council." Joan and Serena watched him rise and walk to the far tipi. The other men who had been sitting there followed him out of earshot of the white women.

"Will he take me to meet his great uncle?" Serena asked Joan.

"I honestly don't know, Serena. If not, I have no other ideas of how you could possibly get home," Joan admitted sadly. "He's your only hope."

He returned to sit gracefully at the fire with Joan and Serena. "I have spoken with council. They feel that there is Great Power at work here, as do I. It is not for us to decide what Spirit Power wants of us. I will take you, Serena, to meet my uncle, Peenaquim. He is the only Great Medicine Man I know who may be able to help you. Let us hope he yet lives when we get there. Come here by sunrise, morning after next with provisions and I will take you to where he lives."

Meeting his eyes with confidence, Serena nodded affirmation, "Thank you, Nawat Sinopa, for agreeing to take me to meet with your great uncle."

Standing, he indicated that it was time for them to leave now. "Farewell sweet Joan. I will see you morning after next, Serena."

The women said their goodbyes and mounted their horses for the ride back to town. The horses walked a quarter mile up the trail and broke into an exuberant lope all the way up the south hill overlooking the valley at the beginnings of Swift Current.

The remainder of the afternoon and evening went by in a flurry of activities and gathering provisions for Serena to take on her journey to the tribe on the bench. Joan thought of everything from a bedroll to gifts. She didn't want Serena out there freezing however long she might be gone; it may be a week or a month.

Serena crawled into bed that night exhausted but excited because she could be going home soon.

SIX
Derek 2012

Well, you give me too much credit for foresight and planning. I haven't got a clue what the hell I am doing.
~ Robert B. Parker

Derek woke abruptly from a nightmare. He had been out in the hills across the creek searching for Serena, she was calling out to him but he couldn't see or find her anywhere. He could hear her but not see her. *What the hell kind of stupid dream is that?*

He quickly dressed and went to the kitchen to make coffee. It was still early, not yet daylight. While the coffeemaker dripped, Derek dressed for outdoors and went out to feed the horses quickly so they would have a chance to eat before he and Jess went for a ride.

Upon his return to the house, Cole greeted him at the door. "Did Mom come home yet? Did you find her?"

Derek was as crushed as his son, "No, son, Mom isn't home yet. But we're going to go out and keep lookin' for her, okay?"

Cole began to cry. "Do you think Mom is okay? Do you think she got dead?" He finally broke down in heart wrenching sobs.

Derek grabbed his son in a bear hug, "Cole, don't do this. Honestly I can't take it. I need to focus on finding Mom. I'm sure she's not dead. I'm going to call Grandma to come spend the day with you while we go out searching, okay? Until we know for sure if Mom's okay or not, let's not jump to conclusions." He pulled back from Cole and looked at his son and smiled. "Let's think positive, that would help me more."

"Okay Dad," Cole leaned in for another hug of reassurance.

"Is Jess up yet?" Derek asked as he poured himself his first cup of coffee.

Cole blew his nose into a tissue as he walked downstairs to see if Jess was up. Several minutes later both Jess and Cole were sitting at the table looking expectantly at their dad.

"Have something to eat, you two. I'll call Grandma and Grandpa to come stay with Cole. Jess you and I are going to saddle up the geldings and go ride along the creek bank and anywhere else where Mom might have gone riding. I know we went out with the quads and trucks yesterday but we might be able to see some tracks and see farther, too, if we're on horseback."

Another cup of coffee was going to be required for phone calls and waiting on the kids to eat.

Fifteen minutes later, Jess was on her way to the barn to start saddling the geldings while Dad talked to Grandma and Grandpa. Cole was a mess and she was glad she didn't have to listen to his whining all day. She was glad to ride with Dad even though she couldn't remember riding with him. Mom always took her riding. What could have happened to Mom that she wasn't home? This was so unlike her.

Jess took Pepper and Slade to the house to get Dad, her spurs clinking rhythmically as she walked. Already there were several vehicles parked in their farmyard. She held the horse's reins in one hand and opened the door with the other, poking her head inside. "Dad, are you ready to go yet?"

"We're coming right out, Jess!"

The geldings followed Jess around to the side of the house to graze on the lawn for a few minutes while they waited.

Jess and Derek mounted the horses and rode north out of the yard. They would ride to one of the neighbor's low level crossings to cross the creek right away.

"Where do you and Mom usually ride in the hills and along the creek when you go out?"

"It depends on how long or far Mom wants to ride. Sometimes we go across here at the neighbor's and then ride north on the other side of the train tracks. And sometimes we ride behind this other neighbor to the east and south along the creek. Let's go the north route first."

Jess let Pepper break into a slow lope as they neared the creek crossing. Meanwhile, Derek was having a heck of a ride on Slade who was not used to his style of riding. Slade was wandering all over the place, side passing and freaking out over Derek's leg cues. Maybe by the end of the day they would have it sorted it out. Slade kicked up his heels as Derek asked for a lope. It looked like a rodeo might take place but Derek was not about to give up. Perhaps he hadn't ridden for some time but that didn't mean he was going to quit. His wife's life might very well be at stake here.

Three hours later they rode back into the farmyard, they had scoured every coulee to the north of the farm along the creek and the railroad tracks as far as Serena usually rode. There was no sign of them or that they had travelled that way the day before. However they did discover an old well up in the coulees and talked about going back there sometime to mark it. Someone could lose a horse in that hole and that wouldn't be good either. They decided to grab some lunch and rest the horses for an hour before they rode the south route.

The afternoon was spent scouring the southeastern creek bank and coulees there, the coulees weren't nearly as long and deep as to the north of the farm. As father and daughter sat upon their horses up on the hill across from the farm, they both felt a sense of pride at seeing their home from this vantage point. Both were thinking of Serena and could understand why she loved riding in the hills so much.

"I think Slade here is getting the hang of me riding him now." Derek remarked.

"Well yeah, Dad, it only took four hours for you to remember how to ride!" Jess rolled her eyes in her head as she turned Pepper south and began walking away.

"Smart ass, isn't she?" Derek whispered to Slade. He smiled because he loved his daughter and wished he had spent more time with her when she wasn't a smart-aleck teenager.

Derek caught up with Jess, "You ride on the top side of the hills and I'll take Slade down into the bottom closer to the creek. Holler if you see any sign that they went this way, droppings or tracks."

"Droppings? Really, Dad!" He got the eye roll again as she turned Pepper toward the top of the hills.

He watched his daughter ride and wondered how and when she had become such an experienced rider. She and the horse moved as one and she rode effortlessly like her mom.

Slade picked his way through the deep grass on the bottom. Derek was scanning the ground for any sign of torn grass or horse manure when Slade exploded underneath him. It felt as though they were 10 feet off the ground and the horse below him was bronc'ing like any rodeo horse he'd ever seen. He shortened up his left rein to crank Slade's head to the side and the bucking subsided to a circle and complete stop. That was completely unexpected, Derek was vibrating. He dismounted when Slade was standing still. Jess loped up to them and stopped a few feet away.

"Holy shit, Dad! What the hell was that?"

Derek was too shook up to say anything about his daughter's language at that moment. "I have no idea what that was about, he just exploded on me out of the blue."

"Good riding, Dad! I thought for sure you were coming off him. I could see daylight under his belly and I was at the top of the hill! We better get your hat."

Derek figured a walk would get some of the adrenaline out of his system so he could resume his ride on this behemoth of a gelding. Slade was a full 16 hands high and weighed in excess of 1,300 pounds. Geez, the gelding's hooves were enormous. He was the biggest Canadian they had on the property. Although he looked as though he should be pulling a plow he really was a nice riding horse, son of a bitch could jump too! Derek led Slade, who looked rather ashamed at freaking out like that, towards where he could see his hat lying in the grass. His hat was way back at the site of the explosion. As they neared the spot, Slade eyed the ground warily when Derek saw the thing he was looking at. A big chunk of sod was turned up beside a long, thick scraggly piece of driftwood. Derek studied the piece of wood for a second and noticed a big wad of black hair on one end of it. With that realization he now recalled hearing a big crack with Slade's bucking fit.

Derek turned to Slade, "You poor bugger, let me have a look at your belly." Sure enough there was some hide missing from Slade's delicate underside, no puncture or blood though. "He must have stepped on the driftwood. Punching him in the belly and that's why he freaked."

"Is he okay Dad?"

"Yeah, he'll be fine, just missing a clump of hair and scared the tar outta him and me both." Derek chuckled.

Derek settled his hat back on his head, "we better keep looking if we're hoping to find some sign of Mom before dark." Derek rubbed the spot on Slade's belly where the driftwood hit him to rub the smack of it off before he mounted to ride.

They continued to make their way southward along the hills near the creek and kept their eyes out for any sign. Deer trails ran every which way throughout the prairie grass before them.

Jess was ahead of Derek on a rise just before a big ravine that ran down to the water's edge. "Dad, I think I found a track," she hollered back at him. He watched her dismount. With a sense of urgency and the excitement of finding Serena he urged Slade to a gallop and reined in beside Pepper. Jumping down he looked where Jess was pointing. "Isn't this Rim's hoof print, Dad?" she sounded hopeful.

His fingers touched the outer edge of the print and sure enough it looked to be the right size for Rim-Fyre's barefoot hoof print. It was about the right depth for his weight with a rider on this type of soil. Derek had some tracking experience because he'd done a lot of hunting when he was younger and out in the river hills with his brothers all the time. Not that he'd ever tracked a horse before. "I think you're right, Jess, no one else rides up here anyway. You and mom haven't ridden up here lately have you?"

"Not for a couple weeks."

"Alright then, let's keep going and see if we can find a few more tracks. You jump up on Pepper there, keep riding this way and I'll follow on foot."

Father and daughter continued on their way along the creek bank near the deer trail that Serena used. Jess found another track but that hoof print was going the other way. Had Serena turned here? Or had she ridden one way first and then the other? They decided to keep going south and then west the way the creek curved to see if they could find more tracks. They found a pile of horse manure but couldn't discern which direction Rim and Serena had been going at that time. They went down a slope and back up and found several deeper tracks, indicating that Rim and Serena had been traveling at some speed. There were even a few spots where the grass had been ripped up. Then onto an open area they followed, where there were rocks sticking out of the ground.

"Dad!" Jess exclaimed. "Come look at this!" she said jumping down from the roan horse. "I think I found something."

More rocks were all Derek could see but he went to look at what Jess found. There was a set of deeper depressions in the grass, as though Rim-Fyre exerted more power here for whatever reason.

"Don't move the horses, Jess. Let's see if we can find any other foot prints or marks near here." Derek continued looking in the grass for any other signs.

"Dad, I'm going to keep going west here, and see if there are tracks further ahead while you look here. That'll be one less horse messing things up here."

After the torn up grass and deeper hoof prints, there didn't appear to be any other tracks going anywhere.

Jess rode back to him. "I rode all the way to the road, there are only one set of hoof prints coming this way off the road. That means mom didn't ride back the way she came and yet we know she rode this way. Did you find anything else? Did she ride straight south of here through the field?"

"I don't know. I can't find anymore tracks here, let's ride straight south in the field and see if there are anymore. If there are any prints, they will be easier to see than in this deep grass."

They criss-crossed through the field to the south of the native grass and were unable to find any sign of Rim's hoof prints. They decided to ride back to the last tracks going west where the rocks were. They could see a quad coming towards them from the Black Bridge road it looked like Dave, Serena's brother. The quad slowed and stopped a reasonable distance from the horses. Derek and Jess rode over to the quad.

"Any sign of Serena?" Dave asked.

"We found some tracks in the hills along the creek. She went this way but from there, no idea."

"I saw one set of horse tracks from the road going this way but none going back." Dave offered. "So what? She just disappeared somewhere over here?"

Derek shrugged his shoulders, it was looking rather unlikely. It was wide open here, not many bushes and there were no tracks to the water's edge. Not like they fell in the creek, besides the creek wasn't really deep enough anywhere at this time of year to lose a whole horse. "We found some sod chunks turned up and some deep depression marks in the grass. Maybe we should ride back over there for another look."

A nod from Dave in agreement as he let Derek and Jess lead the way on horseback. As they rode towards the stones, Derek stopped Slade.

"What is it Dad?" Jess asked riding up beside him.

"Look at the stones from here Jess. It looks like a question mark."

"Ok Dad, I see it. But that's just weird, it's freakin' me out."

"I wonder if this is what I'm thinkin' it is."

"And ... um ... what is that Dad?"

"This might be a medicine wheel."

"Yeah, so what? I'm more freaked out about the question mark thingy. We better ride over there, I think Uncle Dave is getting impatient here waiting." Jess reminded.

They rode closer and dismounted the horses. Dave drove over with his quad and got off to have a look at the hoof tracks and sod chunks that Derek and Jess pointed out to him.

"I don't get it, Derek. My sister didn't just disappear here just because your tracking skills say she did. Besides, it's impossible."

"I think this might be an ancient Medicine Wheel. No one really knows how long they've been here on the prairies or how the Natives used them. Hell, I don't think they know anymore."

"Derek, you're so full of shit! Hell, you would believe aliens came and got my sister! You are such a dreamer and philosopher! You think everything you read is real, it's probably all bullshit! I can see that leaving you in charge of finding my sister is pointless!" Dave ranted. "For all I know you shot her and buried her somewhere!"

Jess jumped on Pepper and galloped off at high speed for the Black Bridge Road. She had heard enough of her uncle's fury and she hated it when Uncle Dave and Dad fought all the time. Couldn't they see they just needed to try and understand each other, get along like a real family? Wasn't the important thing here to find her mom? *Oh Mom, please wherever you are. Come home!* Tears streamed down her pretty cheeks as she let Pepper gallop full out all the way home.

Dave sped off on his quad and left Derek there alone. Words, again they had had words and not very nice ones either. *Why did that asshole always think he was so much smarter and better than me? Besides, who was Dave to think he knew how much I love Serena. She's my wife. I'm the one who's been married to her for 17 years. Damn him to hell!*

Slade seemed anxious standing there with just Derek for company. "Horse, I know you don't know me like you know my wife but you and me need to come to an understanding here. You and me, we're going to become the best of pals here in the next short while and I expect you to work with me. Do you understand a damn thing I'm saying?" *I've lost my mind. I'm talking to a horse.*

A muzzle reached out for Derek's hand. Slade lowered his head in submission as if he did indeed understand. Derek rubbed his forehead. "Maybe you're not so dumb after all." With that said, Slade snorted all over him. "Thanks pal, I'll remember that." He gave Slade another rub for good measure.

Derek walked back to where he noticed that the stones made a question mark formation. Sure as heck he could see it. Then he walked back to the first stone that made the bottom of the question mark. It made a straight path for about six feet and then curved around in a semi-circle. The half circle measured roughly 24 feet in diameter. He continued walking around the outside to see if there was a possibility that it made a full circle and the other half of what he thought might be a Medicine Wheel. Slade followed obediently. Derek had to kick some grass out of the way and pull some grass from around a few stones that he found sticking out of the ground, some just barely there. Half hour later he had exposed enough stones to reveal the other half of the circle and what appeared to be a path from the south leading into it. Wow, this was unlike any type of Medicine Wheel he had ever read about.

Glancing at his watch, he realized Jess had been gone home nearly an hour. Maybe he better head that way too and have a chat with his daughter. No doubt, she was upset with the altercation between him and Uncle Dave.

Slade was more than ready to go. Derek couldn't remember riding a horse that ran as fast as this big black bugger. Damn, who knew he could move like that. Two miles home along the road wasn't as long a ride as he thought it might be. He slowed Slade to a walk down the lane and to the barn to cool off.

Jess was still in the barn and just finishing up chores when Derek rode in. He led Slade into the barn in front of the tack room and unsaddled him there. Slade stood calmly and waited even though this wasn't the usual way things were done around here. Even unbridled with no halter Slade stood in place while Derek gave him a good brushing. "Alright big guy, come with me." Derek motioned with his hand for Slade to follow him through the barn to his pen. The big horse followed and walked right into his pen where hay and water were set out for him. "Good Boy," Derek said as he patted Slade on his way through the gate.

From the barn door Jess commented with a smile, "Way to go Dad, you're becoming quite the horse whisperer."

With the gate firmly latched, Derek turned to Jess. "I'm really sorry about that whole scene with Uncle Dave. He really should be the one apologizing but you didn't need to hear that."

"It's okay Dad," Jess said as she stepped into a hug from her dad. "I just wish Mom was here. I really miss her and knowing that I can't call her is horrible. Call her? Dad, did you try calling Mom's cell?"

"No I didn't, but let's try now." Derek dialed the number from his cellular phone. He held it to his ear, but it just rang and rang. He clicked it shut after the tenth ring. "Sorry Hon, no cell service where Mom is."

Jess hugged her Dad really hard and then let him go. "We'll keep looking, right?"

"You bet! If chores are done let's head into the house and see if Grandma was sweet enough to make us something to eat. After supper you are going to use your super smart brain and computer skills. And then, you and I are going to conduct our own research!"

Derek and Jess walked arm in arm back to the house. Several times Derek winced at the stiffness beginning to set into his legs. He knew darn well it was going to be grim by morning, serve him right for not riding more often.

That night as he lay in bed he whispered to the universe. "If I'm on the right path, send me a sign. Good night my sweet Serena, I love you darling and need you here with me. I don't want to live this life without you."

SEVEN

Travels

*Risks must be taken because the greatest hazard
in life is to risk nothing.*
~ Leo Buscaglia

Too anxious about the day ahead, Serena was up long before she needed to be. All of her provisions were packed at the door, a fire was blazing and coffee was nearly perked when Joan came down the stairs.

"Did you get any sleep last night?"

Serena laughed as she went to take the coffee off the stove. "Not much. I'm too excited, and nervous. I fed the horses already too."

"Oh my, I must have been sleeping like a rock. I didn't hear a thing until Katie woke me."

Joan accepted the enamel mug of coffee that Serena held out to her. They sipped the steaming hot liquid in comfortable silence.

Joan wiped her hand on her beige apron then removed a tattered envelope from her pocket, holding it out to Serena. "You are off to the great unknown today. Neither of us knows if you will be back here or not. If perchance you are not, please deliver this to my parents. If you are, I guess we will find you a job when you return."

"I will definitely do that," Serena said stuffing the envelope in the inside pocket of her brown undercoat. "Thank you for the bedroll, extra clothing, provisions and everything else I might need. You have been so kind and generous, in light of the fact that I don't have a dime to my name."

"Well let's get some breakfast into you and then you can be off."

Rim-Fyre was saddled and packed with enough provisions for a week. Serena didn't think it was possible to pack and tie so much stuff onto one horse but she did it. He waited patiently at the hitching post while Serena went inside to say her good-bye's to Joan.

She kissed Katie on the forehead, "Grow up to be a strong woman like your mama, little one." Joan hugged her fiercely with one arm, "I'll deliver your message when I get there. Take care and have a great life."

"Take care, safe journey. I won't expect you back but if you show up on my doorstep, you're more than welcome." Joan smiled weakly.

The dining room door clinked as she walked through and closed it firmly behind her. Rim-Fyre gave her his familiar 'her-her-her' as she unwrapped the braided reins from the hitching rail, swung them over his neck and stepped into the saddle.

It was still dark out as they rode through the frosty grass across the valley and up onto the south hill. She didn't want to think about home just yet even though it was in that general direction, too, it was too painful. Not even 72 hours into 1887 and already she wished she was home in her own bed lying beside Derek.

A faint hint of light began showing in the east, it wouldn't be daylight for another full half hour. Better to be early than late was Serena's philosophy. They just walked at a leisurely pace all the way to the tiny Indian village.

Only one small fire was burning as she rode into the small camp of tipis. There was no time to dismount or wait, Nawat Sinopa rode around the far tipi on a dark bay roan appaloosa with wild splotches dotting its hind quarters. The sight of this impressive Native man in the early morning light on a horse was breathtaking. He looked like some Native dream god. Buckskin clad with brightly colored beadwork on his shirt and moccasins. Animal furs draped over his horse with several leather bags crisscrossed over his chest. His long black hair flowed past his shoulders and was tied off his face by a headband with eagle feathers in it. He raised his left arm and pointed the way, "Let's ride."

The appaloosa bolted off toward the southwest with Nawat Sinopa's raven hair flowing behind him like a horse tail. Her left hand automatically came forward, laid the rein gently on his neck then with a squeeze and a kiss Rim-Fyre and Serena followed him into the unknown.

The brutal pace did not abate for nearly two miles, up and down the hills and along the banks of the creek past the future site of the Black Bridge Road. Rim-Fyre easily kept no more than four horse lengths behind the Appaloosa. The sun was just beginning to peek over the eastern horizon and cast its bright yellow glow over the prairies as the pace slowed to a walk. Rim was sweating now and blowing a little but felt to Serena as though he might be able to keep that pace for another couple miles. The Appaloosa in front of them revealed that she was a mare as she stopped to dump a load of fresh horse manure right in front of him. Rim didn't even stop to smell the pile as they rode over top of it. Serena was beginning to wonder if she might be looking at Nawat Sinopa's back all day.

Rim-Fyre stepped to the side a few paces so that they were not directly behind the mare and this enigma of a man. Then he increased his pace and gradually worked his way up beside them. Native grass began to take on beautiful tones of yellow and gold as the sun shone its magic fingers across the land. The sky, too, began to take on hues of blue ranging from dark to light as the sun rose higher in the east. It was a new dawn and a new day.

Serena was more than content not to have to talk to Nawat Sinopa for the time being. It was bad enough, having to ride in the company of a Native who looked like a god in the sun, riding an impressive looking Appaloosa, let alone have to talk to him and make any sense. Instead, she focused on the countryside around her and appreciated its raw untamed beauty devoid of farms, fences and telephone poles. If she got home, this memory would be just a dream, so she would appreciate it while she was here.

The sun was warm enough now for her to remove her gloves and stick them in her pockets. Nawat Sinopa looked over at her but said nothing. They rode for another hour before making their way back to a low spot in the creek to stop and allow the horses a drink of water. After drinking deeply from the creek, Rim pawed with his right front hoof for what, Serena was unsure. To splash her maybe, then he mussed his muzzle in the water in play for a few seconds. That was enough of that, she turned him back onto the creek bank and let him grab a few mouthfuls of grass while they waited for Nawat Sinopa and his horse to lead the way.

They continued riding southwest, over hills and through coulees, then joining back up with the creek again. It was becoming a warm and beautiful fall day. Serena shed her overcoat and tied it onto the saddle in front of the pommel along with her bedroll, trying to avoid getting Rim's mane in the ties. The sun was high above them when they stopped near the water's edge. Nawat Sinopa finally dismounted and let his mare graze, he washed up in the creek and Serena followed his actions. He had some pemmican in his bag and sat on a rock and started to eat. A quick rummage through her own pack found a wax paper wrapped piece of cheese, a few strips of jerky along with a crusty bun and some water from her canteen to wash it down. Rim nuzzled her in hopes she would share her bun but he was out of luck today. Serena was famished after hours of riding. Grazing next to her as she sat on the ground, Rim-Fyre kept watch on the man and his horse.

Serena jerked visibly and shot him a look when he finally spoke. "You are very quiet. We will stop before dark to catch a fish for our supper."

After so many hours of only hearing grass rustle, birds sing and the horses snorting and farting, hearing a human voice startled her. *What? She was quiet?* She raised her eyebrows quizzically. "Alright, that sounds good to me."

The wax paper was tucked into her jeans pocket and they mounted the horses and rode along the creek until the banks got too steep and rough. They turned onto a new deer trail and continued straight south for about five miles. Serena gawked around at the landscape. She had no idea where they were, because there were no familiar landmarks for her to gauge their approximate location in comparison to her time. Nawat Sinopa seemed to be paying particular attention to the ground for a few minutes as they rode. The trail went down the length of a deep and long coulee that ran east and west, they were riding west into the bottom of a large valley.

The horses stopped as they neared the bottom of the valley, they could hear rumbling to their right just over a rise they couldn't see over. Rim-Fyre was anxious and perked up his ears, his demeanor changed in an instant. Nawat Sinopa held up his hand, a signal to wait. The rumbling drew closer. When it sounded like it was about to come down on them, the Appaloosa walked ahead. The trail was single file through the bushes to the bottom of the coulee which opened into a valley. By then the rumbling became a small herd of buffalo running about 100 yards from them. Nawat Sinopa only looked back at her, smiled and then rode off with the stampeding buffalo herd. Rim-Fyre felt huge beneath Serena as he proudly raised his head and neck in anticipation of a good run. Serena watched the Native on his loudly colored pony catch up with the herd. "Ah, what the hell Rim, once in a lifetime right?" She gave him his head and leaned forward for his rear and mad gallop to the herd. Rim-Fyre's front feet came off the ground a few feet as he leapt forward with a tremendous burst of speed. Serena leaned high on his neck and let his mane whip in her face as they ran like the devil to catch up with the dark brown shaggy beasts. Rim-Fyre was used to working cattle at home and knew not to rush straight at them but instead to run at an angle beside them. The adrenaline coursed through Serena's lower back and down her legs, this was so scary running beside animals twice the size of her horse, with huge heads and horns no less. Rim-Fyre kept his eyes on the beasts in case one should decide to turn towards them and hook them with a horn. A beaming smile was pasted on Serena's face as they ran for more than a mile the length of the long grassy valley with the buffalo. In the distance she could see the white blanket of the Appaloosa, its black tail flying behind it with Nawat Sinopa holding one arm high in the air. She would have sworn she heard a 'yip, yip, I-I-I-I' along with the pounding hooves of the buffalo.

When the small herd of buffalo took a sharp turn to the right, Nawat Sinopa pulled up his mare and waited for Serena to catch up. Rim-Fyre slowed to a lope and then stopped when he reached them. Both horses were blowing hard and foamy with sweat. As they approached, Nawat Sinopa greeted Serena with the most beaming smile. Her heart almost skipped a beat with the handsomeness of his features when he smiled. She couldn't help the smile that spread across her face. Rim fairly pranced on the spot he was still so full of the action.

"Did you like that?" He asked still smiling.

"Yes! Very much, thank you! Serena exhaled as though she had been running too. She returned the smile to show her appreciation.

"There are not many buffalo left. Most big herds are bone piles across the countryside. Métis pick bones to sell to white men for whiskey."

"We better walk these horses dry." She patted Rim's wet neck as he snorted in agreement.

"Yes, we must ride more miles to get to good place to fish and camp on the creek." He pointed southwest.

Running with the buffalo had done wonders to dispel some of the tension between the two of them.

"You ride as one with your horse." He added pointing a finger at Rim. "What is special horse's name?"

Special, of course Rim was special. A smile accompanied the reply. "This is Rim-Fyre. He comes from a long line of descendants from the first horses sent over the ocean to the French Colonies in the late 1600's. His bloodlines are old and rare where I come from." Serena hoped she hadn't said too much.

"What is this ocean you speak of? You must tell me more."

During the next few hours Serena explained Oceans and as much Canadian history as she could remember, the important stuff. She tried to be considerate of his limited knowledge of the country and what was happening to his homeland now and tried not to mention anything to do with Natives being sent to reserves.

Now that she was here in this time, with this man, she wished that history had been different. She hoped he would somehow escape what she was sure she knew was coming in his future. The miles passed as they rode and talked and without warning they were upon the preselected fishing hole and camp for the night. Serena was more than happy to dismount. She was going to be really stiff and sore tomorrow and tried not to let it show to the man who obviously had iron legs and buttocks. He did not seem phased in the least from the days ride.

The horses were unsaddled and grazed near the creek after they had a lengthy drink of water. Serena left Rim-Fyre's halter on and tied his lead shank around his neck so he wouldn't get tangled in it. He seemed to be content to stay near the camp site.

Nawat Sinopa dug a shallow hole in the short grass, placed a few rocks around it and soon had a fire blazing from driftwood picked up near the creek bank. Plenty of willows lined the bank and with a sharp knife a spear was soon fashioned from a length of it. It didn't seem like more than a sharp stick to Serena when he handed it to her as he cut off another length of willow to whittle one for himself.

Serena eyed the stick then walked over near the water's edge to peer into its depths. The water was fairly shallow here and a few stones peeked from the surface to offer a place to stand. She firmly stepped onto one of the stones and then another to straddle them. The water rippled in its flow around the rocks. Holding her spear she waited for several minutes hoping for a glimpse of a fish.

With spear in hand Nawat Sinopa went further upstream and he, too, found a spot where he could stand on the stones near the middle of the creek. Serena heard the water splash behind her. She turned to see that he already had a fair sized fish wriggling on his spear. *How'd he do that so fast?* She marvelled. As he went back to the bank to clean his fish Serena kept looking into the water. A large northern pike made its way lazily through the stones. She waited until she thought was just the right time to strike as she held her breath. She thrust the spear at the fish missing its mark, drove the stick further into the depths of the water and stones than she anticipated which threw her off balance. Her right foot stomped into the water with a resounding splash. "Shit!" She quickly stepped back onto the rock and made her way back to the bank, her boot now full of water.

Serena sat down on the grass and pulled her boot off to empty it, removed the wet sock and wrung out the bottom of her pant leg. Perhaps she was expecting him to laugh at her, instead now that his fish was on a spit over the open fire, he came over picked up her spear and went back to the creek. Another fish was soon wriggling on the end of the spear he had in his hand. By the time Serena got a fresh pair of socks out of her pack, Nawat Sinopa had the second fish cleaned and spitted over the open fire.

Her wet boot was propped up near the stones of the fire to dry out. A perfect sunset revealed itself in colorful array as the sun disappeared beyond the western horizon. Nawat Sinopa was again quiet as he gazed into the flames of the fire.

The air cooled around them as the sun disappeared in the west. The fire offered heat to only one side. Serena untied her overcoat from the front of her saddle beside her and tossed it over her shoulders. Another pair of socks were located in the pack and she stuffed them inside her wet boot to sop up more of the moisture, it would take hours to dry out her leather boot. Socks aired out later would dry quicker than the leather. She was glad he hadn't said anything or laughed at her for falling into the creek.

Deft hands turned the fish on the spit and added a few more pieces of driftwood to the fire. Serena didn't want to stare at him so she, too, gazed into the fire, hoping for something, what, she didn't know. Her stomach rumbled at the smell of cooking fish.

Darkness settled over the land, Nawat Sinopa determined that the fish was cooked enough for them to eat it. Serena had no experience cooking whole fish over an open fire. She only knew that it smelled good. They had no plates to speak of so the fish on a stick was laid in the grass to cool for a minute. He handed one of them to Serena then began to pick his own meal apart with his fingers, peeling back the skin and pulling the meat from around the bones and eating it. Serena did the same thing, trying not to burn her fingers on the hot meat. Not a fancy meal, no spices, lemon or dill but it hit the spot and the tummy rumbles went away. She couldn't believe she devoured a whole fish. They washed up in the creek and allowed the water to carry away the un-edible parts.

Serena checked her boot, pulled out the sopping wet socks and placing them to dry near the fire. The outside of the boot was beginning to dry from the heat of the flames. Rim-Fyre came over to nuzzle her shoulder so she petted his face for a moment as she sat near the fire. In the span of a few short days Rim made a complete turn around and became a trustworthy companion. He no longer tried to dominate and bite her. This change was good and she wasn't about to look a gift horse in the mouth. Rim went back to grazing but stayed nearby.

Bedrolls were pulled out and placed near the fire but not too close to catch a spark. The wet socks were turned over again to dry on the other side. Exhausted now, Serena crawled between the layers of her bedroll and closed her eyes recalling the run with the buffalo today. No one back home would believe her if she told them. The fire provided just enough warmth as the flames died down to coals for her to fall into a dreamless sleep.

Nawat Sinopa watched her sleep for over an hour before he, too, fell asleep. Although it had been nice to see her smile today after the run with the buffalo and the comfortable comradeship of the afternoon, he was disturbed over the feelings that it gave him. It was difficult for him to grasp all that she said and there were things she was keeping from him. He wanted to shake it out of her and make her say what she knew but she wasn't his, her heart belonged to another in a far off land.

A new day spread its light over the prairies. Serena awoke with a start but dared not move, she could feel a large warm body at her back. Upon opening her eyes she could see Nawat Sinopa lying in his furs across the fire. So, what was behind her? Slowly she pulled her arm free of her bedroll and reached behind her hip to feel this enormous breathing being behind her, it was covered in hair. She turned her head enough to see that it was reddish brown, Rim-Fyre? He rolled onto his breast and just lay there beside her. She sat up in her bedroll so not to startle him and then turned to pet him as he lay near her. How on earth had he lain so close beside her without laying right on her? *Thanks Rim, for keeping me warm last night.* He stretched and rose, nuzzled her and then walked off to graze.

Serena extricated herself from her bedroll, rolled it up and checked her boot by the dead coals of last night's fire. Her boot was mostly dry, only damp on the inside. She put them on to dry out the remainder of the day. The sky was lightening in the east even though the sun wouldn't show itself for a while yet. Dried socks were folded up and stuck back in the pack. She rummaged around, found a biscuit and jerky to chew on as she went to the creek to wash the sleep out of her eyes.

The Appaloosa mare was nearly packed with all of his belongings while he stood there waiting for her to saddle Rim-Fyre. "We should arrive at Uncle's camp tonight."

"Looks like a fine day to ride. Let's go then."

The horses were fresh and eager to go. They loped for a few miles until they reached larger valleys then slowed to walk and enjoy the scene. White tail deer bounded out of bushes in the bottom of the valley as they neared, waving their tails like white flags as they ran off in the distance. They turned west now and were traveling that direction for what seemed endless to

Serena. She had been really stiff earlier but as the miles rode on, the stiffness seemed to melt away.

When the sun was high overhead indicating noon, they stopped at what appeared to be a slough. It was fresh water the horses were eager to drink. Several ducks of varying species flew away at their approach. Bluffs of trees now dotted the hillsides, indicating that they were nearing the bench. The hills were larger and longer leading the way to the Cypress Hills further west.

Serena chewed thoughtfully on a piece of jerky thinking about the hard work Joan put into preparing all the foodstuffs she sent with her. She was grateful for all that had been provided. Grateful even for this strange good looking man that was hopefully helping her find her way home. It didn't matter to her that he was Native, he was still a man and she had no idea how to find her way home by any other means. She had to find out more about the ancient stones that mysteriously brought her and Rim here. What could it all mean?

She broke the silent reverie, "How come you haven't asked me how I got here?" Serena looked directly at Nawat Sinopa from beneath the brim of her Akubra hat.

He looked at her then, "I do not judge such things. We will talk about this with my uncle when we see him. Peenaquim will know what to do with such knowledge."

Serena nodded her acceptance of his answer. They continued on their way. The hills grew steeper as they entered a large and long valley. Deciduous trees gave way to tall pines there and a small brook ran through the bottom. The horses were eager for another drink from the fresh flowing water after they had ridden for so long since the last stop. It felt as though they entered another world down in the pines, it was quiet and peaceful, dreamlike; although it was cooler in the shade of the trees as opposed to the warm sunshine out in the open. A bull elk bugled in the distance. Serena and Rim-Fyre had never heard one before but she knew what it was when she heard it. Rim perked his ears up and neighed in reply.

Even though the trees still displayed brilliantly colored leaves in varying shades of yellow, orange and red, many leaves were already littered upon the ground. There were several large stones rising above the height of horse and rider as they travelled single file down the length of the narrow valley near the brook.

Serena was caught unaware as she heard the scream and felt the blow simultaneously that ripped her off Rim-Fyre's back and slammed her to the ground. All she could think to do as her breath was knocked away and stars filled her head was to raise her arms up to protect her head. An iron like grasp held her well clothed arm as she was pinned to the ground with the weight of the animal that wanted to kill her. She heard thudding hooves near her head and then the weight of the animal was lifted off, leaving her free to roll away. Now on all fours Serena could see that Rim-Fyre had a large, tawny, long tailed animal in the grasp of his teeth. He was dragging the screaming cat away from her and striking it with his lightning fast forefeet. The cougar turned in Rim's grasp on its scruff and lashed out with its front claws on Rim-Fyre's chest. Rim let go of the cat and they eyed each other. The cougar glanced at Serena, met her eyes with his gold gleaming ones, then turned and ran up the hill and through the trees until they could no longer see it.

Serena sat down hard and tried to catch her breath. Seconds later Nawat Sinopa was at her side, still trying to hold his mare and calm her down enough to stand. "Are you okay?"

She turned her hand to look at where the cougar had bit down on her jacketed arm, there was no blood and it felt okay, just like she had it in a vise. With her wind back she might be able to talk now, "I think I'm okay, just shook up a little." Serena rubbed her head where it hit the ground, she was a little dizzy but able to stand and go check on her horse. Rim walked toward her, still running on adrenaline, blood dripping from his chest wounds where the cougar and slashed his hide with razor sharp claws. Serena hugged his head as he placed his forehead to her chest, "Thank you for saving me. I'm sorry you got hurt." She wanted to cry but knew it wouldn't do any good. "Let's have a look here." Inspection of the wounds revealed three deep claw marks on his chest and three shallower marks on his opposite forearm.

"Let us leave this place and go further down the valley, we need to get something on those wounds to wash it and stop the bleeding."

Nawat Sinopa and his mare walked with Serena and Rim-Fyre as they made their way to an open spot near the brook where the water pooled. Serena led Rim into the pool of water, soaked a handkerchief and began washing the blood off his wounds. He stood quietly and let her clean him up. Nawat Sinopa appeared to be playing in the mud he stirred up in the pool of water. When she had the forearm wound cleaned he brought a ball of mud over to her. "And just what do you plan on doing with that mud?" she asked him.

"Cover the wound with it." He held out the ball of mud knowing Rim wouldn't allow him to put it on.

"Are you crazy? That'll just get it infected."

"Put it on," Nawat Sinopa said firmly. "It will stop the bleeding, dry up, keep the bad out and allow it to heal. You need to trust me."

Serena took the cold mud and smeared it into the wounds on Rim-Fyre's forearm and chest. The chest wound required another ball of mud. She added a little water from the brook and made sure that the hair was lying straight around the wound with the mud caked on it. Now it just looked like he had big mud smears on his forearm and chest instead of open bloody wounds. Rim nuzzled her hat while she inspected her application of mud. Maybe it did feel better to him.

"Come, we need to find a safe place to camp for night, we won't make it to Uncle's village today. We will walk and let your horse rest. A walk will keep the stiffness out." Nawat Sinopa indicated with his hand for them to walk abreast rather than single file down the valley.

Rim-Fyre followed Serena without a noticeable limp for most of an hour as they walked to the end of the valley into an open area. A slough with only minimal bushes around it offered a place to camp for night with water and enough sticks for a fire. The sun was making its descent behind the hill to the west.

Too stiff and sore to do anything more than look after Rim-Fyre, Serena watched Nawat Sinopa make a fire. He left for several minutes while the horses grazed and she watched the fire flicker in the waning light. He came back with a grouse which was quickly plucked and cleaned. He washed it off in the slough before committing it to a spit on the fire to cook. The grouse sizzled over the open flames.

While the grouse was cooking, Serena got up and took her handkerchief out. She gave Rim a good rub down to rid him of the sweaty saddle marks and a deep tissue massage all over his body and down his legs, hoping to prevent him from being too sore the next day after fighting off the cougar. Rim closed his eyes in appreciation and relaxed. Hugging his neck she allowed a few tears to escape into his mane. The sleeve of her jacket wiped the rest from her cheeks and she returned to the fireside to share Nawat Sinopa's grouse dinner.

"I'm happy you were not hurt today." He offered in consolation as they washed up in the slough after they ate.

"Me, too." A few seconds passed, "Why did that cougar attack me?"

"I do not know, it is uncommon for them to attack a party of more than one. Perhaps it is Spirits at work. We will ask Uncle tomorrow."

"I feel like I got run over by a buffalo, I need some rest." She wiped her wet hands to dry them on her jeans as she walked back to her saddle to unpack her bedroll.

Rim-Fyre came over and laid down five feet away from the fire with his back to her, she unrolled it beside him and crawled between the layers, snuggling her back against his for warmth. "Good night, Rim." He snorted in reply. Serena gazed through the low fire at Nawat Sinopa while he, too, readied his bed. "Thank you, Nawat Sinopa," she whispered. It was the first time she let his name escape her lips.

EIGHT
Big Medicine

Let our advance worrying become advance thinking and planning.
~ Winston Churchill

Chestnut hide rippled over stiff muscles as they walked slowly the last couple of miles over several sets of hills the next morning. They topped the last rise to reveal a significant sized village in the bottom of the valley. Serena was terrified. Confidence came from close proximity of Rim-Fyre and the will to go home.

Underground springs fed the sizable slough near the village nestled in the wide valley bordered by aspen and birch trees. It appeared quiet and serene. People milled about the tipis conducting their daily routines until they caught sight of the two horses and people approaching from the northeast. Their approach caused a flurry of excitement as women and children ran to tell of visitors approaching.

Before they were within a half mile of the village, two riders came forward to greet them. Nawat Sinopa greeted them warmly speaking their Native tongue. The two young men smiled and dismounted their horses to shake arms at the elbows with their cousin and pat each other on the shoulder in recognition.

"Derek, these are my cousins, Apisi and Dichali." He indicated with his hand as to who was who to Serena. Then he addressed the two men, "This is Derek, we come to seek council with Peenaquim." Both imposing Native men nodded acknowledgement of Serena and said in unison, "Derek."

The four of them turned and led their horses into the village as Nawat Sinopa chatted merrily in his language to his cousins. Alone in the company of the men, Rim-Fyre walked close to her offering his solemn companionship, guarding and protecting her. Serena observed Rim-Fyre as they walked, checking his stride for any shortness in case he should be in pain from the inch deep gashes on his shoulder. The dried mud seemed to be holding well and there was no blood or puss draining from his wounds.

Women and children observed their entry into the village midst, some smiled and waved their acknowledgement to Nawat Sinopa as they made their way to the southern side of the village where Peenaquim's lodge was situated. Others stood with their mouths agape at the stranger who was brought to their village. Serena took it all in as they made their way further into the center of the unfamiliar community, marveling at the ingenuity and master craftsmanship of the tipis which were artistically painted to reflect each individual family and their peoples. Red and black were the dominant colors. Perhaps that was what nature offered most of in terms of natural dye in this part of the country. Deer, elk and buffalo decorated many of the teepee walls and several just had large colored circles painted in a line around the outer perimeter. Rim-Fyre continued to stick close to Serena and guide her direction to follow Nawat Sinopa through the maze of tipis and people milling about in their daily activities.

They approached a hide covered lodge, rectangular in shape with a sloped roof like a lean to shed. A thin stream of smoke rose out of the center smoke hole to drift effortlessly straight up into the sky. There was no breeze to blow it in any direction. An ancient and weathered man with long white hair stood outside the lodge as though waiting for them to arrive. His bright and intricate headband held the hair off of his face. He was dressed in a beautiful butter colored leather shirt and buckskins decorated with brightly colored beads. His plain moccasins appeared worn but well-made. Serena took in the whole appearance of the Medicine Man and to her, he looked like Chief Dan George, a chief and Native spokesman turned actor who had passed on while she was still in school. She was pretty sure he hadn't even been born yet in this time, not for another ten years or so. The cousins dispersed as they neared the lodge waving their farewells to Nawat Sinopa. Serena and Rim-Fyre stepped up beside him as he greeted his great uncle.

The ancient Medicine Man entered his lodge, first indicating for Serena and his nephew to follow. They sat cross legged on the furs piled near the low burning fire.

Nawat Sinopa took his place beside his uncle facing Serena. Their eyes adjusted to the dim lighting, only a sliver of daylight filtered in and around the door flap of the lodge.

Peenaquim addressed his nephew, "My nephew, Nawat Sinopa. I was expecting you to bring this strange white woman to seek my council for I have seen it in a vision. This woman brings us little in her knowledge. We must give her much in spirit, for the future of our people, mankind and the animals the Creator has given us. You must translate for I do not speak her language."

In disbelief, Nawat Sinopa was about to admonish his uncle but thought better of it when Peenaquim reminded him, "Do not question the ways of the Creator, Nephew. You need only concern yourself with assisting this woman on her journey, to do otherwise would only bring you grief."

Peenaquim continued his conversation with his nephew in his sing-song native tongue then turned to Serena to ask her a question.

Glancing at his uncle, Nawat Sinopa translated the question. "Peenaquim wants to know what brought you here?"

Through patient translating and some interesting facial expressions Nawat Sinopa conveyed to Peenaquim the ancient stones placed in a circle with an entrance path and how Serena and Rim-Fyre suddenly found themselves transported back in time. The struggle had been for him to comprehend that she had come from more than a thousand moons after this time.

The wrinkled and weathered face of the wise man showed little emotion as he digested the information while they sat respectfully in silence. Rim-Fyre now nickered his familiar 'her-her-her' looking for Serena. He refused to leave her side and was in complete charge of the situation now standing guard of his own accord outside the lodge entrance. The door flap wavered and flapped as Rim-Fyre nuzzled it with his deft muzzle in an effort to gain some attention in his impatience of Serena's absence.

The ruffling of the door flap caught Peenaquim's attention. Turning to Nawat Sinopa he rattled off excitedly. What was said, Serena couldn't possibly hope to guess. Uncle and Nephew carried on a conversation to which Serena was now baffled and completely lost. Finally Nawat Sinopa directed his attention to Serena.

"Peenaquim feels that your horse has brought you here. Horses are great spiritual teachers and are a symbol of personal power to inspire and motivate us to act in life. In our teaching, horses are believed to be messengers," He paused, "Our ways allow only men to seek visions and often Spirit Animals are shown to us in our visions to assist us in becoming the warriors that the Creator desires for us to become. Peenaquim believes that real animals, like your horse, the buffalo and the cougar are here to teach you on your journey."

"What? Stop! The animals I encounter are pointing me in a direction of my life that I need to learn from and follow? Is that what you're saying?"

Nawat Sinopa looked at Peenaquim and knew that he could tell by her tone of voice that she was disbelieving. Serena was about to get an education in Native American history.

Hours passed in deep discussion and explanation, in the form of old stories passed down from one generation of the People to another. All of the stories involved animals of one species or another, each animal had their place in the universe and had some vital lessons to teach the People. Animals were viewed as wise and powerful and served as intermediaries between human and supernatural forces. Even though the tribal people had to eat and killed animals for food, killing an animal violated the kinship between animal and man. A good hunter who believed and valued his kinship with animals would sing their souls to the land of the dead and thank the Creator for the animal's life that he had taken.

Each animal that Serena had encountered could offer some insight as to what lessons she had to learn and how that might aid her on her journey to find her way back home.

Horses were a symbol of personal power to inspire others and motivate a person to act in life. Upon owning your talents and speaking the truth, you would run towards your dream with joy and grace of the powerful horse. A divine animal that stood for power, stamina, endurance and faithfulness was also a guide to overcoming obstacles. They could also be guardians of travellers to warn of possible danger.

Buffalo symbolized abundance, gratitude, renewing the connection to a higher power. Being thankful would attract more into a person's life. They also represented feminine courage, knowledge, strength and generosity.

Peenaquim felt that Serena's encounter with the cougar was to teach her about the balance of power, action and rest. The cougar's duty was to carry messages from humans to higher spirits because of personal power.

They ate in amicable silence as Nawat Sinopa passed out the remainder of his provisions. Peenaquim placed a pot of water on the coals and tossed in a handful of leaves from a dark, well used leather pouch. Tin cups were procured and hot steaming tea was scooped out of the pot over the fire. Serena couldn't discern the herbal aroma coming from the cup she held to her lips, it was hot and wet, something to both warm her insides and moisten her parched lips.

His large majestic head poked through the lodge flap casting light on the inhabitants within. Rim-Fyre softly nickered 'her-her-her'.

Serena turned abruptly at the call and sternly waved her hand at him to get out. "Rim, no!"

Warm laughter erupted. Peenaquim waved her to go tend her horse as Serena turned to see his large toothless grin. There would be time to talk later. A nod of her head acknowledged her dismissal as she left them to see to her horse.

Rim backed out of the lodge to allow her passage. Purposely walking towards Rim's head, Serena made him back several steps away from the entrance before she annoyingly whispered, "What do you think you're doing?", as she wrapped his head in a hug. The stallion just closed his eyes in acceptance of her presence.

Serena couldn't allow her emotions to show how alone she felt here in this place so she held Rim's head a little longer; hoping somehow he would know how much she was relying on him to get her through this.

The door flap of the lodge opening vaporized the moment. Nawat Sinopa approached them to tell her to follow him to the perimeter of the village.

Nearly submersing his nostrils in the clear water at the edge of the slough, ears moving with each swallow, Rim-Fyre drank deeply. Serena crouched down a few feet from him and dipped her hand to scoop up a drink for herself. It was fairly warm for the end of September and one cup of tea near noon was just not going to cut it. It was quiet here on the south side of the slough, far enough away from the village for a little horse, human solitude. Nawat Sinopa said he would come back for her later this afternoon, give her and Rim a chance for some rest where they were safe.

A quick wash of her hands and face, she dipped the handkerchief in the water and wrung it out to wipe her neck and dry her face. Water was dripping on her back. She glanced back to feel Rim-Fyre drooling the last of the water from his lips onto her shirt. "Thanks buddy," she smiled. Lowering his head to the grass he took a couple of gentle mouthfuls of grass from near her feet.

She inspected the wound on Rim's shoulder which still looked clean with its plaster of dried mud protecting it. Perhaps tomorrow she would wash it out and reapply a fresh coat of mud. Lead rope in hand she turned to walk to a spot that offered better graze for Rim and a drier place for a rest. A suitable spot was soon located that offered a little shade from some bushes and short trees.

She chose a handful of tall brome grass from the tree line and used it as a cloth to rub the saddle marks from Rim-Fyre's back. When the grass fell apart she picked fall-dried prairie wool to rub away any sweat marks and bring a good shine back to his dark chestnut coat. She couldn't remember him being in better shape than he was right now. Rim would require more healing on the claw injuries from the cougar and some good graze before they rode back the seventy-five or eighty miles they had come. Once grooming to her satisfaction was complete, Serena gave him a rub on the neck and walked to the place she felt looked comfortable enough to lie down. She rolled up her oilskin coat and put it under her head and tried closing her eyes.

"You know Rim. I don't know what to make of what was said." She turned on her side propping her head on her hand. "Do you think Mr. Nawat Sinopa is giving me a true interpretation of what Chief Dan George look-alike a-k-a Peenaquim, is really saying?" Rim snorted. "Well most of it was just stories passed on by their culture to explain life I suppose. They are quite beautiful people. On one hand it's really cool to be here in the 1800's and on the other hand it's scary." Serena paused to think about that. "And then there's all that stuff about what animals symbolize. Really, Rim? Are you some mystical creature sent here to teach me lessons? Are you some magical link to a higher power? The Creator, God? Did you just wink at me?"

NINE
Interogations – 2012

*Effort only fully releases its reward after a
person refuses to quit.*
~ Napoleon Hill

"Listen officer, if I've told you once I've told you a thousand times, I had nothing to do with my wife's disappearance. You can polygraph me, give me truth serum or whatever the hell it is you do, but my story isn't going to change. So you can quit listening to my dipshit brother-in-law and quit speculating shit that isn't true. Now, I believe you have no proof of anything and that you can't hold me on speculation. So I'll excuse myself to go home, look after my kids and keep looking for my wife which you are so obviously not doing!" Derek got up from the table and let himself out of the room.

"Don't leave town, Mr. Tattum. We'll be watching you."

Derek's mind was a whir. He hoped Jess's relentless research on Medicine Wheels this week turned up some information he could go on as he turned the truck onto the lane to the farm.

The kids ran out the door to greet him as he closed the door of the truck. "Dad, what took so long? Do the police have any news on Mom?"

"No news on Mom. It looks like we are on our own." He hugged Jess and Cole. They turned to walk to the house. "What did you make me for dinner?"

"Sorry Dad, Jess was on the computer and we just had a peanut butter sandwich. But I can make you a grilled cheese." Cole offered.

With his arms around his kids they walked to the house, "I'll take you up on that grilled cheese buddy, I'm starving."

A fresh hot cup of coffee was in order after the interrogation at the police station. "So Jess, have you been able to find out anything about the Medicine Wheels on the computer?"

"I found out a lot of stuff but I don't think any of it is going to explain or help us find Mom. Dad, are you sure someone didn't just kidnap her?"

Derek looked at his daughter incredulously, "Ok smarty. Then where is Rim? You think they could possibly kidnap him, too?"

"Maybe they kidnapped Mom at gunpoint and made her load Rim in a trailer."

"Honey, you read too much. I know I read a lot of books, too, but with something like this there has to be a reason for someone to kidnap a person much less a horse. I know Rim is valuable but he's not a million dollar horse or anything. Tell me what you found out about the Medicine Wheels."

"I printed off some diagrams here for you to have a look at." Jess handed her dad a binder full of printed material.

With eyes wide in surprise, he took the binder from Jess's hand. "A few diagrams, eh?"

"It's all sorted and cataloged for you to read, there are tabs for different sources. Don't wreck it Dad, I want to use it for a school project later. I mean after we find Mom and all."

Not knowing if he should laugh or cry Derek asked, "Jess, just give me the general gist of the information. I'll read the details later."

"Ok, most of the researchers who documented information on Medicine Wheels on the prairies say that they date from 200 to 3,000 years ago. A large percentage of them have been discovered in Alberta, partly due to Royal Tyrell Museum and digging up all those dinosaur bones and stuff, plus population and well, you know."

Derek only raised his eyebrows at his daughter's description of information. Teenage girls, he wasn't sure if he would ever understand. "Go on."

"So, basically I read a lot of stuff that says they don't know anything about the Medicine Wheels at all. They say it's an enigma, which means ..."

"I know what it means, Jess. It's a complete mystery to all the professionals, too. What about the Natives? Don't they know?"

"The Natives have lost so much knowledge during the past 100 years or more that even they don't know.

Natives currently use the symbol of the Medicine Wheel for spiritual self-awareness or something like that."

"Great. Maybe aliens did capture your mom." Derek mumbled under his breath.

"What, Dad?"

"Oh nothing. How's that grilled cheese coming there, Cole?"

TEN

Pelipa - Lover of Horses

*There is no secret so close as that between a
rider and his horse.*
~ Robert Smith Surtees

Wet horse snot sprinkled her face as Rim-Fyre snorted above her. "Eww! Is that any way to wake somebody up?" She sat up and wiped her face. Noticing the longer shadows of the light and the position of the sun she estimated a few hours had passed while she slept.

"I trust you rested well." Nawat Sinopa said startling her.

"Yes, thank you." Serena gathered up her oilskin coat and picked up Rim's lead rope. "So what happens now?"

"We pack up and ride until sunset to have council with Peenaquim."

"Why?" Serena asked following his brisk walk back to the lodge to get her saddle and supplies.

"There are too many ears here and those who would tell stories. Quickly saddle up, my mare is ready to go and Peenaquim has already left to set up camp."

Rim was saddled and ready to go. There was little activity near Peenaquim's lodge which was set on the far southeast edge of the village. They mounted and rode into the shrubs and tree line right out of camp without encountering a single person.

Golden hues spread across the tops of the trees now covered in shades of yellow and orange while pink and purple clouds painted the western sky with their beauty as the sun dipped behind the horizon. From the hilltop looking into the valley they could discern a small thin stream of smoke wending its way lazily into the air a faint breeze blowing it easterly. It was a gorgeous fall evening.

With the horses unpacked and hobbled for the night, Serena and Nawat Sinopa sat down at Peenaquim's fire. This was a place he must have come to frequently. A lean-to frame shelter was constructed into the southern hillside and only required a few hides thrown over its frame to make it habitable. The valley was situated east and west which allowed maximum daylight into the shelter and warmth from the southerly winter sun.

Strips of meat sizzled on the spit over the small open fire and a bowl of orange berries were at the old man's right side.

The other two horses hobbled away from the immediate camp to graze but Rim-Fyre preferred the close proximity of his person.

Tossing a few more sticks on the fire, Peenaquim told his nephew to go fetch more firewood for the night.

Serena was alone with the old Medicine Man who seemed to peer into her very soul as he looked at her. She was unable to tear her gaze away from his scrutiny. Saying nothing, he turned his attention from her to the exquisite example of a stallion that stood a few yards behind her.

Ears perked forward as Peenaquim spoke to him. Rim nodded his head or snorted in response to this one sided conversation.

Serena dared not turn to look at Rim but watched the wise facial expressions and listened to the old man's voice as he spoke to her horse. Dusk was well past and the skies continued to darken with night. A handful of stars sparkled their attendance as weathered hands raised heavenward and Peenaquim sent his prayers to the Creator.

The fire popped loudly as the prayer came to a close. The resounding silence seemed eerie to Serena after what she had just witnessed. It was profound and special and yet she had no clue what just happened.

The lithe form of Nawat Sinopa returned to deposit a large armful of suitable wood near the fire. He asked if the meat was ready to eat. The spit was removed and the elder passed out a portion of meat to each of them.

Handing Serena the bowl of berries, Nawat Sinopa said, "The buffalo berries are very sour but add good flavor to the meat."

The meager meal was enough to satiate hunger and was eaten in silence.

Serena boldly asked Peenaquim directly, "What do I have to do to get home?"

Nawat Sinopa quickly translated her question.

Peenaquim stood up and answered, "The night and my dreams will tell me." Then he walked off to his shelter for the night.

Her gaze fell to the fire disappointed, *'were the answers in there?'*

"Aurora."

For the first time Serena really looked at Nawat Sinopa. His skin was smooth with handsome features. She wondered why he was here guiding her instead of with a wife and family. Turning to follow his gaze to the northern skies, they observed the blue, white and green lights dance their way across the north. *'Did this mean something, too?'* Serena doubted that she would ever see something so magical again.

When the light-show calmed and ended they sought their bedrolls near the warmth of the fire and closed their eyes for a night of rest.

"Heya, heya, heya, hey."

Soft singing and chanting woke Serena from the most restful night's sleep she had since her arrival to the past. Sitting up in the dim light of early dawn to ascertain where the singing was coming from, she turned to see Peenaquim standing with arms spread wide to the pre-dawn purple light in the east. She sat up and listened as she rubbed the remaining sleep from her eyes. The song was reverent and soothing like balm to a sore. On he sang until the sun's rays reached over the tips of the tree line to cast warmth on the land of a new day. The silhouette in the light of dawn lowered his arms slowly then turned to approach the fireside.

So enraptured by the morning song, Serena hadn't noticed that Nawat Sinopa built a fire and was boiling water for tea.

Seed gruel was served for breakfast along with a handful of dried berries which Serena ate with gusto. Serena made use of a small spring-fed waterhole situated nearby. Rim accompanied her and drank his fill.

It was time for some answers.

Through patient translation, Nawat Sinopa told Serena that Peenaquim's vision was that the Old Ones had come to speak to him. The circular stone formation with a path was not made for man alone, but was a passage for animals. The Creator had given it to them as a gift. The Old Ones said that Serena must listen to the animals because they pass through the stones at will but do so only on the full moon. Serena's horse Rim was a Great Spirit and could determine her path home but even he must wait for the full moon. Serena was to return to the stone passage and seek her vision there. Peenaquim and Nawat Sinopa were only messengers to teach her some of the old ways and the reverence of animals before it was all gone and the animals would be no more.

He went on to say that the blood of animals will wash mother earth at the hand of man. Serena must connect with the animals and feel their pain for soon their time shall come. The Creator will give them revenge and man will pay.

"Peenaquim says you are now named Pelipa (Pell-ee-pa), lover of horses. If your heart is pure, your horse will take you home at the next full moon, if not, you will wait. You must fast for three days when you return to the stone passage, seek your vision there. Let your vision guide you. An eagle will visit you. I can tell you no more, you will leave at dawn." And with that Peenaquim sought tea and rest.

ELEVEN
An Eagle & a Gift

The manner of giving is worth more than the gift.
~ Pierre Corneille, Le Menteur

Serena took her leave and went to spend time with Rim-Fyre, resting or grazing. She put his bridle on and went for a ride bareback allowing Rim to pick his way on whichever deer trail he chose. She took in the scenery of the land, the open prairie hills, stands of short trees, mostly birch and aspen.

Full moon, but wasn't the full moon tonight? If that was the case how could Peenaquim's words be true? Serena and Rim had come back in time the day before the fall solstice, a week ago, or, what day was it? Serena was conflicted. There was so much to think about. How could she possibly figure it out? If only Rim could talk.

Serena's mind wandered at will from what Peenaquim had said to what she had to do, how she felt about all of that and what Derek and the kids might be doing.

How were they coping with her disappearance? Would she ever see them again? With her thoughts all a jumble she completely lost track of time and where Rim was taking her.

She regained her focus and realized that Rim had taken her to the base of a rocky outcrop surrounded by huge pine trees. *Where did they materialize out of?* At the base of the rocks sticking out of the hillside was a pond with fresh clear water in it. A small trickle of water seeped out from the cracks in the rock formation to form a pool at its base. Rim stopped in the deep green grass near the pond for a drink of cold fresh water. Serena dismounted. It was sheltered here in the shade perhaps that was why the water was so clear. Serena could see the small stones and pebbles that naturally lined the pond. The air was cooler and felt like a Holy Place. Serena crouched down to scoop up a handful of water while Rim was sipping water and could see their clear reflections in the pool.

The whooshing sound of heavy wings beating the air broke the quiet. Serena looked up to watch a giant bald eagle alight with a soft rustle in the pine tree not far from her. The eagle was imposing, regal and watched her with great intensity. Rim was unaffected.

Serena shivered, not from cold but from the sense of something that was about to happen. Perhaps in reverence, Serena stayed kneeling as she kept a close eye on the eagle. Serena could feel the eagle in her heart and mind, talking to her, as if it were an everyday occurrence.

Pelipa, my daughter, lover of horses, lover of all animals, I am Sky Spirit. In the coming days you will grow in spirit in ways that you never thought possible. You must always stay close to the spiritual truth or terrible things will happen. You will gain the ability to see hidden spiritual truths and the knowledge of magic. Before you leave this place you must accept a gift from the Old One. In return you must bestow a gift upon him, to show your respect and gratefulness for his vision. The majestic eagle turned his beak to his tail feathers and plucked one white tail feather and dropped it to flutter softly to Serena's knees. Then he turned his beak to his right wing and plucked one dark wing feather and dropped it to land beside the first. *Give the tail feather to the Medicine Man as a gift. Keep my wing feather close to your heart, to remind you of spiritual truth. It will give you the speed of an eagle in flight. Farewell Pelipa.* The great wings spread wide and the magnificent bird hopped once and flew off to the west into nothingness.

Serena blinked and her mind was clear of the eagle's thoughts with his departure. She looked down at her knees at the two eagle feathers. One dark and one light, she gently picked them up, felt their warmth and tucked them gently into her shirt for safe keeping. *Did that really happen? Am I dreaming?* Something special just happened. The eagle called her Pelipa just as Peenaquim said earlier and an eagle had indeed come to tell her something. Serena wasn't sure just how she felt about that yet.

Rim waited patiently while Serena stood up and walked over to him. She hopped on his bare back with ease and allowed him to take her back to camp. Rim broke into a smooth ground covering lope, executed effortlessly.

By the time they returned to camp the sun was sinking below the horizon. Serena set Rim free to graze for the night and gave him a hug before she walked back to the fireside to retrieve her jacket. It was cooling rapidly as the sun descended. A prairie fowl carcass was spitted over the fire where Nephew and Uncle sat in quiet revere. The roasting bird smelled good.

"How was your ride?" Nawat Sinopa asked.

Sitting down by the warmth of the flames Serena replied, "Very good, thank you."

"Your horse appears well rested and ready for the return journey. We will leave at first light."

"That sounds good to me."

"Are you hungry? This grouse is ready to eat." He smiled.

Bones was all that was left of the grouse. Peenaquim quickly stashed the bones into a leather pouch which Serena presumed was for soup later.

Wise eyes observed her with interest. It would soon be time to bid her farewell.

Serena went to the spring to wash up after eating and scrub her teeth with a wet handkerchief. She knew she smelled like horse sweat and longed for a warm bath. She returned to the fire where only Nawat Sinopa sat, and spread the kerchief out to dry.

The Medicine Man returned from his shelter with a large bundle in his arms. Nawat Sinopa translated the old man's words to Serena. "In our land, our ways are to exchange gifts. I am giving you this buffalo robe to keep you warm at night in the days ahead. May the Spirit of the Great Iinnii (buffalo) give you strength and courage for the challenges you will face."

He held the buffalo robe bundle out to her for her to accept. Serena held her arms out to receive the robe. When he placed it in her arms she was surprised at the great weight of the hide. She nodded in respect to Peenaquim and said, "Thank you." *The Eagle Spirit was right.*

One eagle feather hardly seemed like a fair exchange for the beautifully tanned and cleaned buffalo robe. Serena had very little with her in the form of possessions. She opened her saddlebag and reached in to see what she could possibly give to Peenaquim along with the eagle feather that was tucked in her shirt near her heart. The first thing her fingers encountered was her stainless steel, no leak travel cup. She forgot all about it until now. It would have to do. She set it down on the ground before her and reached in to find the eagle feather with the square-ish end. Serena pulled the silvery-white eagle's tail feather from her shirt and stood up to present her gifts to the Medicine Man.

Tanned and wrinkled hands accepted Serena's gift. Peenaquim's faded brown eyes met her light-blue ones. "Pelipa, fly with the swiftness of Sky Spirit. Bless your vision so that you might return your family so far away. May your great horse take you far in life. Heya."

They sat down at the fire for evening tea before they turned in for the night. Peenaquim was asking Nawat Sinopa questions and looked puzzled at the bright blue travel cup Serena had given him.

"Perhaps I should show Peenaquim how the cup works." She smiled.

The cup was handed to her. Unscrewing the lid she asked Nawat Sinopa to put some tea in it for

Peenaquim. Then she put the lid back on, showed him how to depress the catch to open it to allow the liquid to pass through. She dumped a little tea on the ground to show how it worked, then depressed the catch and took a drink and passed it back to Peenaquim. It took a few tries before he figured out how to tip it back to his mouth and depress the release lever at the same time. Once he had drunk his tea out of the cup, he smiled and nodded his approval at Serena. Serena explained that it kept the drink hot, much longer.

The old man nodded happily at hearing this translation from Nawat Sinopa. "You wouldn't happen to have two of those in your saddlebags would you?" He enquired with a smile.

As they drank their evening tea, Serena watched the old weathered man gently run his fingers over the eagle feather. She wondered if he felt its warmth and magic, too, as she could feel the feather near her heart under her shirt. He looked up at her gaze and nodded his gratitude and approval of her gift. She could only smile in return and run her hands graciously over the soft buffalo hide on her lap. Serena wondered why neither one of them asked her where she got the eagle feathers from. *Did they just magically know?*

Peenaquim rose and bade them good night, "Rest well and safe journey, Pelipa."

That night Serena laid the bundled buffalo robe near her side as she crawled into her bedroll. It, too, held a thrumming-warmth and she fell fast asleep to the sound of beating wings and pounding hooves.

TWELVE
Troubles

Adventure, yeah. I guess that's what you call it when everybody comes out alive.
~ Mercedes Lackey.

Serena woke to the sound of Rim snorting repeatedly near her. Obviously it was time to get up. Nawat Sinopa, too, was now awake. They both noticed that Peenaquim had packed up and left on his own horse some time ago. No longer did hides drape the lean-to frame and only the appaloosa mare and Rim remained in the pre-dawn light.

Their breath was visible in the brisk morning air and steam rose from the small spring.

Cold breakfast was in order and Nawat Sinopa discovered that his uncle left a bundle of provisions for them to take on their journey. He brought Serena some jerky and hard biscuits to chew on while they packed their horses.

Rim did not seem to mind the added weight of the buffalo robe in addition to the saddle, bags and bedroll that Serena tied on his back.

Bright rays soon streaked across the sky as the sun made its appearance over the eastern horizon.

Serena marveled at Nawat Sinopa's agility as he grabbed a handful of his mare's sparse mane, jumped onto her blanketed back, all without messing up his gear. His provisions were either strapped onto his horse's neck or his back and shoulders.

The short statured trees and occasional meadow gave way to short bushes and shorter grass interspersed with sagebrush as they continued on their way northeast towards Swift Current.

Raising his head, Rim noticed them first, a small band of riders coming toward them from the northwest. Quickly pointing out the riders in the distance to Nawat Sinopa, Serena asked, "Should we be worried about them?"

"Out here, one must always be wary. Trappers come and rogue Blackfoot or Métis on the run. It would be best if they do not see us."

It was too late. They could already see that the riders were heading directly for them.

Rim-Fyre's demeanor changed in an instant and he rose up to his full height, stallion on guard. Serena just knew that the men approaching them at a hard gallop were bad news. The appaloosa mare became antsy as well.

Looking at her companion with concern, she asked. "Do we make a run for it?"

Nawat Sinopa lowered his left hand in a stay calm gesture, "No, our horses are fresh and they've just run theirs for half a mile to get here, but they might have long rifles. We will save our horses and not risk getting shot in the back."

Laying her hand on Rim's neck to calm and comfort him Serena spoke in low tones, "Just keep calm, buddy, and save it if we need it. It might help if you acted like a plug instead of the proud and beautiful stallion you are, you know. You would appear less valuable to those who would like to steal you from me." Rim snorted his disagreement at her words.

"Follow my lead if things go wrong," were the last words Nawat Sinopa spoke before the riders thundered up to them.

Rim-Fyre reared at their abrupt approach. There were four of them, yanking on their horse's mouths to stop them from running headlong into the rearing red stallion. Two of them were grisly white men in their thirties and the other two were Métis, so distinguished by their chopped black hair and white man's clothing. The long dark haired white man with a beard obviously the leader was big and shaggy looking in his dark woolen coat covered in greasy residue. Serena saw they carried rifles in scabbards on their saddles.

The dark haired white man directed his question at Serena, assuming she was in charge because she was white. "Now where are you off to, young feller?" He crossed his wrists over his saddle horn in a relaxed manner and spat brown tobacco juice onto the ground.

Her chest felt hot with the pounding of her heart and the serious reality of the situation in which she now found herself. Serena mustered up the strength and courage to say, "My guide here is taking me back to Swift Current to head back east before winter."

"Oh," he said with amusement. "Where you comin' from?"

Serena had no idea where the words that came out of her mouth were coming from as she heard herself say, "I delivered some documents to Corporal McDougal with the North West Mounted Police in Fort Walsh. Not that it is any business of yours."

The man was taken aback at her forward manner and brusque attitude so Serena took full advantage and jumped right in with, "And sir, just who might you be and why are you interrupting my journey?"

He shook his shaggy head as he readjusted his hat remembering that he had a force of rogues with him, still at an advantage. "I'm Trapper John and you're trespassin' here."

Rim snorted audibly over the huffing horses they had ridden in on. Serena observed that the horses had no specific traits of any breed she was familiar with but were rather plain looking.

"Well now, Trapper John, I had no intentions of trespassing or setting up shop here, we're just passing through. So if you'd excuse us and let us pass we'll be on our way."

Nawat Sinopa sat his horse in awe of the matter-of-fact tone Serena carried out as she spoke. He had no idea she was capable of such assertion because she'd hardly spoken a word to him all day. He did, however, notice each twitch of every man mounted before them. They were itching to do something and were just waiting for the signal to go ahead with orders.

"Well, wet behind the ears lad, I don't know yer name and that's some fine horse and gear you got there. I'll be relievin' you of yer possessions here shortly."

Serena didn't even bat an eyelid, "Not bloody likely, John, it'll have to be over my dead body."

"As you wish." He replied reaching for the handgun in his holster.

His hand barely touched his colt as Rim-Fyre rushed his horse biting the gelding in the knees and slamming him hard with his shoulder. Serena grabbed for her stock-whip and flung the whip out as an extension of her arm smacking the rogue's hat off, cutting his ear. His gelding fell to its knees, taking his rider by surprise. Losing his balance, he grabbed the saddle horn taking his horse down with him.

Nawat Sinopa took the stallion's cue and flew into action. Tomahawk in hand, he quickly dispatched the first Métis, catching him completely off guard. The second rushed his mare with tomahawk at the ready. A swift backhand from Nawat Sinopa sent the second Métis' tomahawk flying. The men grappled one another as the two of them tumbled to the ground. More lithe and agile and not under the influence of alcohol, Nawat Sinopa soon subdued the second man with a hard blow to the head.

The younger white man was charging forward to aid his buddy, Trapper, who was now securely stuck beneath his horse, too exhausted and injured to rise off of his rider. The movement caught Rim-Fyre's eye and he snaked his head around biting the chestnut mare the man was riding in the jaw, sending her in retreat from his aggression. Serena cracked her whip over his head narrowly missing him as he reached for his gun. Nawat Sinopa was now on his mare running for the back of the last thief facing off with Serena. He leapt off his horse grabbing the man at the waist to pull him off, the two of them hitting the ground with a thud. The mare now rider-less, ran to avoid another bite from Rim. While Nawat Sinopa was fighting the white man on the ground, Serena dismounted and picked up the colt .45 that Trapper had dropped. She cocked the hammer back and walked over to him trapped under his horse. The brown gelding screamed in terror at Rim's approach but the stallion's fight was not with him. Serena saw that the gelding's front leg was broken as she neared.

Trapper shouted at her, "Get this damn horse off me!"

Keeping her distance from Trapper, she turned to see Nawat Sinopa rise and walk to his mare. Three men lay dead at his hands. Rim stood and waited.

Turning back with a steely glare she said slowly, "No, I will not be getting this horse off you." Serena was getting mental flashes in her head of this man shooting buffalo by the hundreds and leaving them to die a slow painful death. "No! I am going to end the suffering of this horse as my gift to him. And you are going to stay under his carcass until the coyotes come and eat you, or you die a slow agonizing death."

She ignored his ranting and screaming at her as she knelt down to stroke the geldings face. He blinked and softly blew his understanding. "Shh, it's okay, good boy. You can go to your rest now."

She aimed the .45 at his forehead, half way between his eyes and his ears and squeezed the trigger. Rim jerked at the resounding shot.

Silent tears rolled down her cheeks as she watched the gelding exhale his last breath. Reaching down she gently closed his eye with her hand.

Trapper laid there, his face red from screaming, his hair even more disheveled, writhing in the grass. "Shoot me, too!"

"Sorry pal, I can't kill a man and nature's not done with you yet. You will pay for the atrocities you have committed." She turned to Rim, picked up his reins and began walking toward Nawat Sinopa and his mare.

"Wait!" Trapper shouted. "What's your name?"

Serena turned around, "Horses know me as Pelipa. Now you can go to hell."

Together they walked, leading their horses away from the carnage in which they had been forced to partake. An hour later they found two of the horses, Serena ground tied Rim, caught them, relieved them of their tack and set them free. The horses had earned their freedom. Scars marked their thin bodies. With good graze and no one to bother them, they would regain their weight and make it through the winter.

The sun would be going down in another hour so they mounted their horses and rode for a while. Neither one of them felt like talking. They came upon a reliable water source and stopped to camp for the night.

Serena gathered some dead wood from the base of a few small trees that grew near the water's edge and started a fire. Then she unsaddled and unpacked Rim to let him graze.

His horse now unpacked, Nawat Sinopa slumped to his bedroll near the fire Serena tended. "Who is Corporal McDougal?" he asked.

Serena looked at him and smiled, "Someone I made up. I didn't know you had a tomahawk, and thanks for saving me."

"Your horse saved you. He is a good warrior."

Looking at Rim with admiration she agreed, "He is a good warrior, and so are you. Are you okay? You look at little pale."

Grimacing now, he disagreed, "Not pale, still Indian; sick and hurt maybe. I twisted my knee in the battle."

His swollen knee was discernible through his buckskin pants as he rubbed it gently. "Might have a broken rib or two."

"Is there anything I can do to help?"

"I need to … prop up my leg … and find … some way … to lay … sit. I can't … lay down." His speech was coming out in short bursts between breaths. He was in a great deal of pain.

"Well you were fine just a few minutes ago, what happened?"

"I … don't … know … hurt." He huffed.

"Is there anything I can give you for pain?" she asked.

"In my pack …" he breathed.

Serena got his pack, taking his items out near him. When she got out the right pouch he stopped her. "Make tea," he said placing the pouch in her hand.

She placed the small pot filled with water on the hot fire. While the water boiled, Serena made a backrest for Nawat Sinopa with her saddle and pad then propped his knee up with her buffalo robe. He was shivering so she covered him with his woolen blanket. The tea was foul-smelling but he drank three cups of it anyway. It seemed to make him more comfortable. They shared some of the provisions from his pack and the last piece of cheese that Joan sent with Serena. She had no ice pack for his knee so Serena improvised by putting her cold wet handkerchief on it to help with swelling.

The fire burned low. "Rest well," she said watching Nawat Sinopa drift off to sleep. Rim grazed close as Serena sought her bed in exhaustion. Closing her eyes, she heard the joyful yipping of a pack of coyotes off in the distance.

THIRTEEN
Painstaking Journey

A path is made by walking on it.
~ Chuang Tzu

It was well past mid-morning before Serena and Nawat Sinopa were anywhere near ready to mount up and ride for the day. The foul smelling tea seemed to help ease Nawat Sinopa's pain some but he was still limping around and short of breath.

"Do you want me to build a travois and haul you back to Swift Current?" Serena attempted to joke.

Nawat Sinopa was not happy with her suggestion, "No! Do you have any idea how much riding in one of those bumps you over the gopher holes? I'm better off on a horse." He added emphatically. "Can you help me on my horse now?"

"I suppose." Serena helped him up on the offside of his mare.

They walked the horses three or four miles before Nawat Sinopa was asking to stop for more tea. Serena stopped and helped him dismount. They found a waterhole and driftwood for a small fire to boil the water. The provisions provided by Peenaquim would last until the morning so they shared the sparse provisions and saved some for noon the next day. Once the pain tea was boiling and Nawat Sinopa began to feel its benefits, they mounted up and walked slowly for a few more miles. By Serena's best estimate they only made another five miles before Nawat Sinopa looked green and ready for more pain tea. It was mid-afternoon and Serena felt that they were not getting very far today. The slough they found was a poor water source. She hoped boiling it would purify it. A full pot of water boiled on the fire Serena made, while the horses grazed and her injured companion rested. She made the tea and handed him a cup then poured the rest into her canteen. Serena surmised that Nawat Sinopa could drink cold tea on route until they could find a suitable place to camp. Her anxiety at the time wasted during these two hour stops was making her nervous and she didn't want to risk running into any more trouble.

The area they were riding into began to take on a familiar appearance as the day was coming to a close. The Swift Current creek lay around another valley and up the next set of hills. Even though the Indian scout was exhausted and in pain, he complained little. Rim-Fyre offered his steady companionship and chose the flattest possible route.

They topped the hill and were elated at the sight of the creek ahead. Serena loped Rim ahead to find a suitable place to camp while Nawat Sinopa slowly walked his mare there.

Rim was grazing peacefully while Serena tended her already blazing fire. Her saddle and pad already propped up, a ready resting spot for Nawat Sinopa when he came. She was about to go find a willow branch to manufacture into a fishing spear when he rode around the bushes. Rim nickered a greeting at their approach.

"Ready for a rest?" Serena asked rhetorically. She gently took his mare's bridle in hand and led her to the fire to assist his dismount. Serena swiftly un-blanketed his mare and let her go graze. Nawat Sinopa had been unable to carry his packs on his back and shoulders today so Serena and Rim-Fyre had carried it for him.

Once she had her injured companion comfortably seated in the makeshift chair she made fresh tea for him from the water already boiling in a pot.

"Thank you," he offered. "It's my ribs causing all this pain. Maybe after I drink this tea you would have a look at it for me?"

Other than assisting him on and off his horse, she found the thought of being in such close proximity to him disturbing and more intimate than she felt comfortable with. But then again, if it was something she could adjust, they might be on their way quicker than the snail's pace of today.

Cup now in hand, he smiled and nodded his thanks, raising the steaming tin to his lips. His nose wrinkled as he inhaled the distinct odor of the tea.

Serena turned to grab her already made willow spear and walked to the creek. Both horses backed themselves from the muddy creek bank with dripping muzzles at Serena's approach. She walked upstream from where the horses had disturbed the water to search for a fishing spot. There appeared to be no good place to get to the water's edge without slipping in so she walked back to where the horses had been drinking in hopes that the water had cleared.

Several sizable stones protruded from the water nearby. Serena was able to use the stones as a step to get further into the center of the creek where the water was a foot deep or more. The water ran clean and clear, over a gravelly bottom. Two of the stones were the right distance apart for Serena to set her feet to balance herself. The breeze rippled the surface of the water as she gazed into the depths hoping for a glimpse of a fish. Ten minutes went by with no sign of one but she did notice more than a dozen sizable crayfish swimming around. She had never eaten crayfish but heard that some folks referred to them as freshwater lobster. Abandoning her post she went to get the only pot they had from the fireside. She poured the remaining tea in her canteen for Nawat Sinopa and took the pot back to the creek with her. He watched her quizzically.

Serena rolled her sleeves up past her elbows, rinsed her pot, put a little water in it and resumed her post on the stones in a crouching position. Peering into the surface she slowly submersed her free hand into the flowing water. With a quick strike she pinched her fingers behind the snapping front claws and netted herself a three inch crayfish. She plopped it into her pot.

When she placed the third crayfish in the pot, she thought of her son, Cole. How many times had he asked her to play in the creek and catch crayfish with him? Too many. And too many times she said, 'no, I'm too busy.' Tears welled up in her eyes and blurred her vision. "So sorry, Cole." She murmured, wishing she could hug her boy right now and tell him that she loved him.

With fierce determination to get home and go crayfishing with her son, she wiped the tears with the back of her free hand and caught several of the clawed critters. There was no way she was eating more jerky and pemmican today. She was having lobster for supper, with or without butter.

Nawat Sinopa cringed at her suggestion of eating the boiled crayfish. Maybe he thought he had to eat the shell so Serena pulled them apart with her fingers until she broke through to the white tail flesh. He ate some and was mildly impressed to discover that it was edible after all. It was steaming hot and it was good. The best thing she had eaten for days. Serena enjoyed every bite of her freshwater lobster supper and tossed the shells and leftover bits back into the creek when she went to wash up.

"Now, you look at ribs?" He asked when she returned to the fire.

"Um, sure, I guess." She tossed a few more pieces of driftwood onto the fire so it burned a little brighter in the diminished light.

Nawat Sinopa lifted the right side of his buckskin shirt as Serena crouched down near him to have a look at his ribcage. He smelled of horse and leather. She turned her head to have a look at his ribs, there was some bruising there but it looked as if one rib was huge. To the best of her knowledge bones didn't swell, it was muscle, tendons and ligaments that swelled when damaged.

"Ok, this rib looks funny. I'm going to touch it and see if I can feel if it's broken or what's going on with it, ok?"

His dark brown eyes looked at her and then quickly dropped back to his side, "Ok." He was uncomfortable with direct eye contact with her as well.

Reaching out her right hand to gently touch on the surface of his skin, he jumped from the touch of her cold finger tips, she jumped too. "Shit, sorry," she said.

Nawat Sinopa laughed and grimaced in pain. "Try again. I'll try not to jump this time."

Serena placed her finger tips on his ribs again and ran them up towards his sternum, then back down towards his back. It felt like one rib was crossed over another so she felt again to see if she could discern where it began and ended. Sweat began to bead on Nawat Sinopa's forehead.

"Sorry, I think you have one rib crossed over another, I can feel it. The one rib needs to be pulled down off of the other in order to give you any relief. I don't know if it will fix itself."

"Ok, do it." He said.

"I wish I had something else to give you for pain. Do you want more tea?"

"No, I'll have more tea after. Maybe give me a stick to bite on so I don't yell. It's going to hurt like hell."

Serena found a suitable short, clean stick in her pile of firewood for the evening. He stuck it in his mouth and grabbed the edge of his bedroll then nodded his head.

In order for Serena to push down on the rib that was crossed over, she had to reposition herself crouching down behind him. Holding his right shoulder with her left hand she could push down on the crossed rib with her right thumb. Instinct was all she had to go on. She firmly grasped his shoulder with one hand then set her thumb firmly on the rib that was sitting on top of the other. She hoped this would work and not injure him any worse. Rising up on her knees for more leverage, she tapped his shoulder to let him know she was going to do it. He grasped the bedroll tightly as she pushed down on the rib. It felt somewhat flexible but the muscles were holding that rib firmly in the wrong place. She pushed harder and could feel it begin to move, his shoulder feeling like a rock beneath her hand.

She could feel him break out in sweat beneath her hand, it beaded everywhere on his body and yet he did not cry out. When the green branch in his mouth snapped in half, he slumped forward, unconscious. Serena pulled his limp body back towards her and continued pushing with her thumb. With his whole body relaxed now, the rib slid off of the other one back into place. Serena laid his muscular body back in the semi-reclining position against her saddle, then ran her hand over his ribcage to make sure that the rib was all the way back where it was supposed to be. Satisfied with her adjustment on his ribs, she covered him up with his shirt and a blanket. He appeared ashen in color. If he didn't come to in fifteen minutes or so she would try to wake him. His breathing was shallow but regular and he still had a good pulse. Serena knew that much from taking first aid courses in the past.

Feeling like she needed to move around and go talk to Rim for a few minutes, she stood up and tossed a few more branches onto the fire. In an hour or so it would be glowing coals again. It took a few seconds away from the firelight before Serena could discern Rim-Fyre grazing nearby. He lifted his head when she began walking toward him so he met her half way, placing his muzzle in her hands. Serena ran her right hand under the long heavy mane on the left side of his neck and felt the warmth of him in the cooling evening air. Rim nuzzled her left hand even though she had nothing to offer him in the way of treats.

"Rim, I am ready to go home." He snorted in answer. "I miss Derek and the kids and I need my family, too." Rim lowered his head so she could rest her forehead near his ear. "I hope I'm not going crazy. Having eagle's talk to me and all is a little out of my league don't you think?" Rim snorted emphatically. Serena gazed upward to the stars, it was clear this evening and they seemed extraordinarily bright. It was beautiful and serene here but it still wasn't home. Hugging Rim around the neck she whispered, "Take me home, soon, please." She turned and walked back to the fire to see if Nawat Sinopa was conscious.

He was still out like a light but Serena noted that his color was better and his breathing seemed easier, perhaps he was even breathing deeper than she had noticed all day. She left the canteen of tea near his side and turned into her own bedroll.

Serena could feel the ground tremble beneath her feet as she stood in the sea of buffalo, they ran past and around her, she could see nothing but brown and black shaggy hides and the dust from their hooves was choking her. She woke up coughing and sputtering from the smoke blowing over her from the coals of last night's fire. She sat up trying to find her way out of the smoke and get some fresh air.

Nawat Sinopa was not in his bedroll but came limping toward her from the edge of the creek bank carrying a pot of water. Serena stood up as he dumped the water on the smoking coals to douse them.

"No breakfast this morning?" she asked.

"It's going to be windy all day today so we better ride and hope we find shelter soon."

"Alright. You feeling any better?"

"I can breathe today and only my knee hurts now. Thank you."

"You're welcome."

Both horses were packed and ready to go. Serena had to do up her choke-strap on her hat to keep the wind from whipping it off of her head. The wind was becoming stronger and cold enough for her to put her long oilskin coat on overtop of her layers and jacket. She was thankful she had it with her.

The wind was at their side most of the day depending on the direction the creek was flowing. They were using it as a guide back to Swift Current. With Nawat Sinopa's ribs feeling better they were able to lope for short periods of time allowing for more miles traveled in a shorter span of time. The wind was incessant and increased in velocity as the day wore on. Clouds began moving in from the west indicating a big change in the weather.

The horses were thirsty so they stopped at the creek to water them and refill their canteens. They walked for a mile or so, sharing the last of the pemmican and jerky Nawat Sinopa had left in his pack.

The temperature continued to drop during the day, so they began looking for a suitable sheltered place to stop for the night. A valley presented itself late in the afternoon. They had to ride deep into the bottom of the coulee at the base of the trees before they were able to find a place sheltered enough for a night's rest. Relief was evident on the horses as they entered shelter from the horrendous wind.

The horses were unpacked and tied where there was sufficient grass for them to graze. Several thick broken branches were used to construct a lean-to in the hillside and leaves were gathered to make a cushion on the ground. Serena's buffalo robe covered most of the lean-to frame to provide maximum coverage from the elements. They were hoping it wouldn't snow just yet.

The wind was strong enough down in the bottom of the coulee that they couldn't risk a fire. They hunkered down sitting in close proximity to one another to preserve body heat this night. The remainder of their woolen blankets covered them over their clothing. Both were too exhausted to even murmur good night. The wind blew soughing in the trees, lulling them to dreamland.

FOURTEEN
Return to Swift Current

I'd rather be on my farm than be emperor of the world.
~ George Washington

There was nothing left to eat. They packed up their woolen blankets and Serena's buffalo robe as the first few drops of rain fell with a pit-a-pat on her hat in the morning fog. Last night's wind was nothing more than a bad memory.

The horses were wet. Water ran off the brim of Serena's hat as she tied her bedroll to the saddle. She slicked water from the seat and quickly mounted Rim to prevent any more rain from falling on it. Final adjustments were made to her oilskin coat to cover her legs and most of the saddle. Nawat Sinopa looked rather dashing as the light rain thoroughly soaked him. He looked even more wild and untamed with his black hair wet and sticking to his smooth brown face. She wondered how he could possibly look more handsome. Then she banished those thoughts before they became something else.

The footing was still good on the wet grass in the hills but they quickly loped to flatter terrain. It was difficult to ascertain but the light fog indicated an all-day rain.

They were wet and hungry, quite miserable actually. Food and shelter were of utmost importance but so was getting back to Swift Current by nightfall.

Rim was eager to go this morning, he felt fresh and rested. Serena allowed Rim-Fyre to lope at a steady pace for quite some time before she slowed him to a walk. Nawat Sinopa caught up and allowed his mare to walk beside the stallion as the steam rose off the horse's necks. The Appaloosa mare slipped in the wet grass a few times while Rim-Fyre walked sure footed as if he were on dry ground.

It was peaceful and serene in the late morning fog and rain. The landscape around them was partially obscured and softened in the haze of the cloud. The only sound was the pit-a-pat of the rain on Serena's hat and oilskin coat and the rhythmic footfalls of the horses hooves. Thankful she was dry but at the same time, she felt sorry for Nawat Sinopa because he must be soaked to the bone in his buckskins. They rode side by side at a walk for several miles while they allowed the horses to snatch a bite of grass here and there.

"We will be at Pile of Bones by dark," Nawat Sinopa announced.

"I thought the terrain looked familiar. That's good. At least we will have a dry bed to sleep in tonight." She smiled.

The fog lifted the further north they travelled but the rain did not let up. It was a gray and dreary day.

Her mind was a whir. There really was nothing to politely talk about with Nawat Sinopa and besides it seemed like the wrong thing to do. Talk business or facts, perhaps, but just general small talk seemed far beneath the aura around him. Serena spent the remainder of the afternoon deep in thought about her course of action as soon as she arrived back in Swift Current.

Familiar hills presented themselves and the horses sensed their nearness. Without being asked the horses picked up the pace and began to jog. The grass was slippery, hooves churned up grass clods as the pace continued. Rim broke into his ground covering slow lope and held his pace. Serena felt as though she was sitting in a rocking chair and allowed Rim to lope as Nawat Sinopa's mare trotted along beside them.

"I would like it if my horse had that slow gallop," he said clinging to the mares back with his knees.

Serena just smiled but slowed Rim-Fyre a short while later as they approached the creek crossing to ride the last few miles to Swift Current. Daylight was waning and they were both anxious to get off their horses and fill their bellies with food. It had been a hard day's ride.

Nothing looked more welcoming than the tipis of Nawat Sinopa's small village. Serena would have to ride an additional two miles to bunk in at the C.P.R. Dining Hall with Joan and her family.

They stopped where they would go on separate paths. "Say hello to Joan for me and stop in for tea before you go to seek your vision, Miss Serena. It was an honor to ride with you and your spirit stallion."

"I will. Thank you, Nawat Sinopa, for the experience of riding with you and meeting your uncle, it is not something I will soon forget. Heal quickly." She added.

He nodded his wet head towards her in farewell and looking like a god himself, he waved as he said "Heya!" and rode off down the hill toward the tipi village.

"Farewell!" Serena shouted back and turned Rim-Fyre up the last hill to Swift Current.

Bone weary, Serena let Rim lope at will. He knew his footing on the slippery prairie grass and his own limitations. He also knew where they were going. Gravel crunched under his hooves as they approached the C.P.R. yard and the small barn there. Serena let herself and Rim into the barn and put him up in the spare tie stall. She wanted badly just to lie down in the straw herself and go to sleep but she pushed herself to unsaddle Rim-Fyre, feed and water him. Rim was content to stick his nose deep into the hay manger and eat his fill. Serena gave him a long, hard hug on the neck. "Thanks, Rim, rest well tonight. I'll see you in the morning."

Saddlebag and buffalo robe in hand, she walked out the barn door into the gray wet dusk. The supper hour was long over but she was sure that Joan would have something for her to eat in her well-stocked kitchen. She was famished!

The door clanged its welcome as Serena walked in the dining hall. It didn't take two minutes for Joan to come down the stairs to see who in tarnation was at her door at this hour of the day. She rounded the corner of the wall to see Serena standing there dripping water everywhere.

"Hey, Joan, I made it back." Serena announced taking off her wet hat. Her bags were set at the doorway.

Joan's beaming smile welcomed her, "I thought you were going home?"

"Well I am, but I can't go yet. In the meantime, could I get a sandwich and a coffee? I haven't eaten anything all day."

"Hang up that wet coat and get yourself into the kitchen. I'll see what I can whip up for you." She waved Serena to come around the corner to the kitchen.

With her coat and hat hung up at the door, Serena walked around the stair wall into a brightly lit and fire warm kitchen. The dry heat from the stove was just what she needed to drive the cold out of her bones. Joan had a kettle on for coffee and was in the dumbwaiter gathering supplies to make a sandwich.

Serena went to stand by the stove and soak up some of its heat. Her oilskin coat and hat had managed to keep most of her dry today but the bottoms of her pant legs and boots were wet and would require a thorough drying. Some dry socks might be in order too.

Joan set a huge sandwich on the butcher block in front of Serena and wrinkled her nose. "Whew! You smell like a horse and a wet one at that. I'm going to run upstairs and tell Mac we're down in the kitchen here for a while 'til you dry out and warm up a bit. I'll be right back and bring you some dry socks and slippers. Get those wet boots off, barefoot would be better than that," Joan admonished as she flew around the corner and up the stairs.

Serena went over to the basin and poured some water from the bucket so she could wash up. Joan's homemade bar of soap smelled fresh and clean as she soaped up her hands and face. The water was cool but it felt good to wash some of the grime off. Just washing with creek or slough water for over a week was good but it lacked the clean of soap. Once she was freshened up, Serena went to pour a cup of coffee and sit down to eat the sandwich that Joan made for her. A simple meat and cheese sandwich but to Serena it was the most delicious thing she had ever eaten. The coffee was a nice chaser. Joan came around the corner of the stairwell with her hands full, just as Serena popped the last bite in her mouth.

"I brought you a change of clothes." She said setting the clothing on the chair by the stair wall. "I'm going to heat up another kettle of water and you can change and wash up in the storage closet under the stairs."

Only then did Serena notice the cloth draped short doorway on the stair wall she was facing. Her back was to the stove and the heat coming off it felt way too good. As Joan was setting the full kettle on the stove Serena went to wash up her sandwich plate, snatching a mouthful of coffee as she did so.

Joan turned to her, "So, can you even go back home?"

Serena turned to her as she was drying the plate, "I met with Nawat Sinopa's uncle, Peenaquim. You know, he looks like Chief Dan George," she said smiling. "He told me so many stories about spirit animals and said that Rim-Fyre is magical and can take me home on the full moon. But I have to fast and seek a vision and do what my vision tells me to do before Rim will take me home." Serena put the plate on the shelf in the cupboard and turned back to Joan. "I'll do whatever it takes to get home, Joan. I miss my family and right now I miss a shower and my own bed most of all." She tried to force a smile out of her weariness.

"So, there's a good possibility you can go home?"

"Yes. I'm going to have to go out there to the stones and spend some one on one time with my horse to figure this all out. Right now, I'm just about too tired to think." She reached for the mug and had another sip of coffee. "Thank you Joan. This is the best coffee I ever had the pleasure of drinking. It's heavenly."

Joan smiled. "I am happy to see you though."

Serena washed her hair in the basin first and towel dried it before she went into the storage closet with a warm bucket of water and soap. She undressed in the semi-darkness and quickly washed with soap and a wash cloth. The towel was rough against her skin but whisked away the excess moisture. A few minutes later she stepped out of the closet into the warm kitchen dressed in clothes a few sizes too big but fresh and clean.

The women sat in chairs near the stove while Serena's hair dried and sipped on another cup of coffee. It was long past dark while they burned kerosene in the kitchen. Serena filled Joan in on the most exciting parts of her journey to and back from Peenaquim's village.

Joan closed up the kitchen, stuffing more wood into the stove before they took the remaining lantern upstairs with them.

Serena lacked the energy to undress. She covered herself with the quilt on the bed and fell fast asleep as her head sunk into the down filled pillow.

Serena rode Rim-Fyre through the thick fog, walking, ever walking. Up ahead she could see a figure walking, too, but she was unable to make Rim-Fyre go faster so that she could see who it was. The figure stopped and called out, "Serena-a-a-a!" She knew it was Derek but she had no voice and she could not make Rim-Fyre take another step toward him. 'Why, Rim? Why won't you take me to Derek?' But the dark chestnut stallion just reared in refusal ...

Serena awoke to loud banging on her door. She jumped up, made her bed and went down to the kitchen for coffee. Joan was already in the warm kitchen with three lanterns lit for light. It wasn't even daylight yet.

"Morning," Serena offered groggily.

"Morning," Joan replied. "What are your plans for the day?"

"I need to rest and wash my clothes I guess. Is the coffee ready? I really need to wake up. I could have slept much longer."

Joan laughed, "You can go to bed earlier tonight, I won't keep you up so late. And besides you won't have to ride a horse all day if you don't want to."

"Right, I'll have a sip of coffee and run out to feed Rim." Serena walked over to the stove to check her boots that were drying there all night. They were dry so she pulled them on.

Joan poured two cups of coffee and got out her supplies for breakfast. "I only have a handful of customers this morning so a small breakfast today."

Serena had a few mouthfuls of coffee. "I'll help you peel potatoes and then while you're frying breakfast I'll head out to the barn to feed Rim. How does that sound?"

"Works for me!"

A few minutes later three skillets were sizzling on the wood stove, Serena went to the door and put her coats on. It was brisk out this morning and the rain didn't seem to be letting up any. She donned her hat and stepped into several puddles on her way to the barn.

'Her-her-her' greeted her as she opened the doorway to the barn. She left the door open for light as Rim turned his head to look at her. "Hey, Rim. You hungry, buddy?" He neighed shrilly in answer. Serena chuckled to herself as she forked hay into his manger. Denali was still munching his hay in his tie stall on the other side of the aisle from Rim. Serena grabbed the wooden bucket and went outside to dip water from the rain barrel. Rim drank deeply from the bucket that she offered him. Serena gently stroked his neck while he drank. He slobbered his thanks over her hand when he was done and went back to eating his hay. She patted his rump as she walked out of the tie stall. "I'll be back a little later, buddy. Enjoy your breakfast." She left the door open a crack for some fresh air, the barn would need mucking later today too.

Joan was dishing up plates in the kitchen when Serena returned. She washed up in the basin.

The doorbell clanged its welcome as someone walked in the dining room door. Joan whisked out with the coffee pot to seat her guests. Several more were heard clomping down the stairs. Serena scooped some fried potatoes onto the plates on the butcher block that were already loaded with eggs and a slice of ham. Joan returned for the plates and took them out to her customers. They made more coffee and enjoyed a cup while they waited for more water to boil.

Customers paid and left. They sat down at the butcher block table and ate breakfast. Katie cooed contentedly in her basket. A large pot of water was boiling for washing Serena's clothes. The women chatted amicably while they washed up dishes from breakfast.

A large wash tub was hauled out of the storage closet under the stairs. Serena had been too tired last night to notice it. A wash board was placed in the tub and a bar of soap. Joan poured a bucket of cold water in the tub and then added the kettle of hot water to it.

"There you go, now you can wash your clothes. I rinse with cold water."

Serena looked at the tub and board. "I've seen one of these in a museum before. I can only guess at how it works." Then she laughed. "Alright, here goes nothing."

Serena took her cleanest clothes, undergarments and long johns and placed them in the water then she rubbed the soap into the material and gave it a scrub on the board. Wrung it out by hand and set it aside for rinse later. She washed her filthy jeans last. Her hands were angry red and hurt after she wrung them out once. Together the women carried the washtub to the kitchen door and tossed the brown water out onto the ground. Rainwater was carried in to rinse the clothing and it was wrung out again and hung to dry on a makeshift line strung across the kitchen. The jeans were hung closest to the stove and even then, it was some time before they began to dry.

It was time to get ready for lunch. Joan prepared most of the ingredients for the huge pot of soup that was now bubbling merrily on the stove, spreading its aroma throughout the room. The women prepared sandwiches to go with the soup. An hour and a half later lunch had been served and cleaned up. Serena was exhausted from working in the kitchen all morning. She was ready for a nap.

Joan got a leg of lamb from the icebox and placed it in a large roasting pan. She seasoned it and placed garnishes all over it before placing it in the oven. It appeared to Serena that she was expecting a large crowd for supper.

A nap was just what Serena needed. She felt rested and ready to do something for the rest of the afternoon. Her clothes were still drying. Joan went with Serena out to the barn to find an old canvas tent in storage. They spent a half hour brushing their horses, time well spent.

That night Serena went to bed as soon after supper as she possibly could, she was completely exhausted.

The fog was thick as she rode Rim-Fyre towards her farm, she could see a figure walking ahead of her and again, they were unable to reach the figure. "Serena-a-a!" he called. She was unable to call back and again Rim-Fyre refused to catch up to the figure. She knew in her heart it was Derek. 'Why won't you go, Rim? Why? Why? Why?' And once again the powerful stallion reared in answer...

FIFTEEN

Visions

Knowledge is love, light and vision.
~ Helen Keller

Joan hugged Serena fiercely. "I wish I was going with you."

"I know. I'll be back by the weekend to spend Thanksgiving with you." Serena broke off the hug and turned back to Rim-Fyre who was now all packed with a tent, her saddle bags, bedroll, buffalo robe and a canteen. She had enough food packed for one good meal before she came back from her fast and vision quest. Hard as it was to help Joan with breakfast, Serena managed to begin her fast today with only a cup of coffee.

It was going to be a lovely fall day and hopefully the sun would dry the still wet grass and muddy puddles.

Joan waved her good-byes as Serena rode Rim-Fyre south toward her future. Serena was as eager as Rim-Fyre this morning so she squeezed her legs on his sides and asked for a lope. Even though they were churning up mud in their wake, Rim-Fyre gave no sign that he was running on anything less than perfect footing. It was more than a mile to the top of the hill near the Knight property. Mrs Knight was out in her yard enjoying the sunny day and waved to her as she rode by.

To the southeast Serena could make out the tiny tipi village belonging to Nawat Sinopa but that wasn't their destination today. She turned Rim straight south towards the spot on the creek where their ranch would be in the future, their future. It seemed as good a spot as any to camp out for the next few days and was within easy riding distance of the Medicine Wheel if she felt the need to go there.

Rim walked and slipped a few times on the wet grass on the way down the other side of the hill. Serena kept her seat and balance with his steps. It was second nature now to allow her body to flow with his movements after all of the miles they had ridden in the past week to the bench of the Cypress Hills and back. This was a short ride of only a few miles to their destination. It would be a great opportunity to be alone and think without any interruptions. Serena was looking forward to the next three days.

The brilliant sun was warm as they made their way across the hills south of Swift Current. Serena took in the landscape and mentally compared it to what it would change to in the future. A deep sadness came over her as she realized all that had been lost in the changes that the future would bring this place. What good had possibly come from the innovation and change that the European's brought to the new world? It was beautiful just the way it was. No wonder the Indians had fought so bravely to keep what they had always known in living within the wonders of nature. It was profound to realize this. Perhaps that was part of the reason that she had been sent back in time. She was only one person and Rim-Fyre was only one horse, together they could not alter the entire future of the Indian Peoples or the country as a whole. Not that she wanted to mess with that anyway. It was a matter of acceptance on her part for what the future would be.

Rim stopped of his own accord at the creek bank of their future home site. Dismounting, she left the reins on Rim's neck and walked around on the bank, searching for what, she didn't know yet. Rim walked behind her like a dog. Further south along the slope were several trees clumped together, Serena saw the beaver swimming downstream from them, lazily churning the waters with its large flat tail. Small birds took flight from the trees as they approached. This was a good place to set up camp there was plenty of driftwood debris from the previous spring flood near the water's edge that could be used to make a fire.

"Well, Rim, what do you think? Should we make camp here?"

Rim's hairy forelock bounced as he nodded his head and let out a long wet snort. Serena smiled taking that as a yes. "Alright then, let's get this gear off you."

Camping gear and tack removed, Rim-Fyre wandered far enough away to find a suitable place to roll in the drying grass. Serena found a fairly level spot near the trees which still held their golden leaves to set up the two man tent. Basically it was just a tarp and several stakes were used to prop it up at each end. There were two tent poles that fit together that made the top portion of the roof. There was no floor in this tent so Serena had to pick the grass to a shorter length. The ground beneath was still damp from the rain but sunlight beamed into the tent entrance drying it out. Another canvas sheet was placed over the grass in the bottom of her tent to keep the moisture from soaking into her coverings and woolen blankets. Her saddle, camp supplies and buffalo robe were placed in the tent corner.

 Now all that was left to do was to clear a spot for a small fire pit. There was a tin bowl in her pack which she used to scoop out the soft wet dirt and grass for a shallow pit. Scraping the grass from a perimeter of a foot all around where her pit would go would prevent sparks from starting a grass fire. Serena pulled the grass around the perimeter another foot to a shorter length, no tall grass was sticking out anywhere around the fire pit. The last thing she wanted to do was start a prairie fire. Although right now, the ground was saturated with two days of rain. It would dry quickly with the sandy soil that was typical of that area of the prairies. A few rocks placed around the perimeter of the shallow depression would contain the fire and hold heat long after it died low. A hot rock wrapped in a cloth could keep you warm for quite some time.

 The sun rose higher and warmer indicating it was near noon. A few gulps of water from her canteen satiated her hunger so she could go in search of rocks. Rim-Fyre grazed nearby lazily flicking his tail. She watched the ground surface for any hand sized stones that would make suitable fire-pit rocks and found several that were not imbedded in the soil. For the few that were, she kicked them easily from the wet ground. She was thankful for the rain the previous two days otherwise the turf held the stones as though they were set in concrete. With her arms and hands full of all the stones she could carry, she walked back to her camp to place them. Only half enough, she went walking the other direction north along the creek bank and up on the flat. Serena was pretty sure this was where her pasture would be in her time and there were always stones out in her pasture. The second armful of stones completed the circle of rocks around her pit. She sat for a few minutes and deliberated getting some sticks and driftwood collected for a small fire later tonight which would ease the chill of the evening air.

Making its way across the hemisphere, the sun warmed and dried the prairies. It was late afternoon before Serena was happy with her stock of firewood. She kept busy all day and would sleep well tonight.

Rim walked up to her and offered her his back. Without a second thought, Serena grabbed his ample mane with her left hand, placed her right on his withers and threw her leg over his back. It felt wondrously different sitting atop his muscular back with fabulous thick wavy mane on his neck in front of her and no saddle between them. She marveled at his small foxy ears, how they barely poked out of all his mane and forelock as she ran his silky rain washed mane through her fingers. Life truly looked better from the back of a horse and Serena was coming to realize that Rim-Fyre wasn't just *any* horse.

Rim walked from the small camp on the creek bank and across the open prairie toward the west. *Had it only been over a week since she'd come here? Never in her wildest dreams did she think that her spit-fire errant stallion would be ridden bareback and bridle-less and yet here she was doing just that. Allowing him total freedom, they weren't even in an enclosure of any sort. It was just a woman, her horse and the wide open prairies - no fences, no holds barred.* Serena allowed that feeling to hold her, live in the present, this present moment being truly free on Rim-Fyre with only their emotional and mental bond holding them precariously together. This was faith.

The muscles bunched and contracted beneath her buttocks and legs in the familiar way of a change of speed as Rim-Fyre transitioned from a walk to a slow lope. Serena rode him as effortlessly bareback as she did with a saddle, completely in harmony with his rocking gait. The sun was making its way to the western horizon but wouldn't be dark for a few hours yet. Surefooted, Rim loped over the hill. A slight breeze and the momentum of loping lifted Rim's mane to fly around her on either side of her body. Feeling complete faith in her horse Serena sat him proudly and raised her arms out to the side to feel the breeze. She closed her eyes, raised her face sunward and smiled. Opening her eyes again, she put her hands on her thighs as he continued his loping pace for some time westward across the prairie, missing each stone and gopher hole by altering his stride. Serena knew by the feel of the muscles in his back that Rim was going to slow down to a walk. She adjusted her body position, no indication of losing her balance as he did so. Then he stopped at what looked like a rock pile facing the setting sun and bent his head to graze. Serena just sat on him scanning the horizon for any sign of wildlife and took in the beauty of the scene before her. It was familiar, she had driven this way many times but it was even more stunning without any fences or buildings in the distance to mar its raw beauty.

"Besides this gorgeous sunset and this romantic scene, was there anything else here you wanted me to see?" she asked Rim.

He shook his head from side to side in answer as his heavy mane flopped back and forth over his neck falling to the left side. "Well thank you for bringing me here to see this, it's beautiful," she said stroking his shoulder affectionately with her right hand. Rim-Fyre grazed for a few minutes and looked up to the south. Serena couldn't see what it was that caught his attention. Then he turned back and took up his lope again all the way back to Serena's tent on the creek bank.

Serena slid off his back when he halted near her tent and gave him a hug around the neck. Rim-Fyre hugged her back, wrapping his nose around her waist. That ride had been the most exhilarating experience of her life. The sun dipped behind the hill leaving an orangey glowing sunset to complete the day.

Serena assembled sticks and dried grass in the fire pit and used one of the wooden matches from her pack to light it. No wind hindered the flame so the dry grass burned long enough for the kindling to catch fire. Once it was burning with some heat, Serena added a few larger sticks until it burned hot. She drank some water from her canteen and basked in the warmth from her little fire. Rim stood quietly nearby not running off anywhere, just offering his quiet solemn presence.

It was quiet out here, only the sound of the burning wood popping broke the silence of the prairies late at night. She heard every footfall Rim made stepping through the grass, the occasional snort, a bite of grass, everything. She was hyper sensitive to sound. A few crickets survived the frost and voiced their bleeping song. And the sound of the evening breeze rustled the tall grasses and dry yellow leaves in the trees overhead. Serena laughed when her stomach growled angrily. Somehow that sound didn't mesh with what she was listening to. She drank more water to quell her hunger. With no food in her stomach now for 24 hours since her meal last night at Joan's, she got cold sooner and was beginning to feel less energetic than she had all day. The larger pieces of wood were still damp, she listened to them hiss and spit when she tossed them onto the hot coals.

Gazing deep into the fire she let her thoughts run home to wonder and worry about Derek, Jess and Cole. Her heart ached in misery. They were as far away as death to her, here in this alternate time. She had to hope that her vision, providing she even had one would show her the way home and that it would unfailingly work. Tears slipped down her cheeks as she sat there missing them, wishing she would have said or done things differently. Hugged her children a little closer and told Derek that she needed to be close to him, love him for all time. "Don't give up on me, Derek, I'll find a way home. Somehow …" She wiped her eyes with the back of her jean jacket sleeve and watched the smoke rise up to the stars, "I'm going home! I don't know how yet but you can't keep me here. My husband and kids need me and I need them. Please help me get back. Show me the way."

A full body shiver went over her. The fire died down enough that it was safe to close her weary eyes and rest. She laid out a woolen under-blanket on the canvas in the open-ended tent and used her saddle pad for a pillow. She lay on the length of wool and covered herself with the buffalo robe which was just the right length and width to cover her adequately. She gazed over the fire and into the starlit sky until her eyelids gave way to fatigue.

Feeling the intense warmth of the bright sunlight on her face, Serena awoke. The coals from last night's fire were cold but the air around her was warm. She was more than willing to shed the heat and weight of the buffalo robe. Serena neatly folded her blankets and robe then scanned her surroundings for the whereabouts of her horse. Rim-Fyre grazed a hundred feet away. She yawned even though she felt well rested. A drink of water and washing in the creek did wonders for waking up and quelling hunger.

Serena dawdled on the creek bank, watching the sunlight glare off the ripples on the surface of the water. The diamond bright light played on the rise and fall of the ripples as she watched a single muskrat poke its head through the surface of the water nearby. It paused long enough to recognize that it wanted to go beyond the place where she crouched near the edge, swimming further toward the opposite bank and downstream from her.

Rim drank upstream from her and she watched the sunlight reflect on his coat causing it to gleam on the upper curves of his shoulders and hindquarters. Serena stood up and shook her legs out because they were tingling with numbness from kneeling too long. The stallion lifted his dripping muzzle from the bright rippling water to acknowledge her.

Today seemed like a good day to go have a look at the Medicine Wheel, she hadn't been there since the day they came through time. Serena went to get Rim's bridle. He followed her and stood with his head low so she could place the bit in his mouth and fasten the crown piece behind his ears. She tossed the reins over his neck and leapt onto his bare back with ease. Using only her leg cues and weight to turn him they went south along the creek to find a suitable place to cross. Rim-Fyre pushed through the willow bushes on the edge of the bank, following a deer trail that lead to the water's edge. The water level here was low so he picked his way across the stony bottom. Long grass and cattails greeted them on the other side, the mud sucking at his hooves as he stepped up onto the dry bank.

An easy jog took them the half mile to the place on the other side of a hill where the stones lay. Walking over to the stones that were faintly visible Rim stopped and waited. Serena dismounted and tied the reins around Rim's neck so that he could graze unencumbered by them. There was really nothing distinct about the stones before her so she walked around them looking from different angles. Some were large and stuck out of the ground nearly a foot, while others were barely discernible. Nothing stood out to her. She began to pull the grass from around each stone finding that it was harder to pull the prairie wool out than she thought it might be. Her hands became raw and sore from the tough blades of grass. She put her lined gloves on, which helped some. Thirst overcame her after an hour. Serena neglected to bring her canteen with her. Rather than riding Rim-Fyre to the creek she opted for a short walk to the flowing water to quench her thirst.

As she returned to the Medicine Wheel from the creek she could now discern the complete shape of the stone formation that she had so arduously labored to uncover from the prairie grass. It was an open circle with a pathway into it from the south. Eleven stones made up the circle like a clock and an additional two stones from the seven and five o'clock positions or one and eleven depending on which way she looked at it, made up the pathway. Fifteen stones in total. A clock? Time? This made her mind whir at an incredible dizzying speed. She sat down in the grass.

A soft muzzle rubbed on her left shoulder. It was time to go back to her camp now. She mounted Rim-Fyre and looked hard at the plainly visible Medicine Wheel. A clock, the realization was overwhelming. Rim turned north of his own accord while Serena went along for the ride. Before she could fathom what just transpired, Rim had returned her to camp. It was nearly sundown. *But how did that happen? Where did the time go? Wasn't it just noon? Her mind was playing tricks on her in her weakened state of fasting, or was it? Was this part of her vision?*

Rim-Fyre was unbridled and free roaming, Serena managed to light a fire and drink an entire canteen of water in attempt to maintain her sanity. She was so hungry and tired but refused to give in and eat the food that she knew must be eaten on the fourth morning to break her fast. It was only one more day. Serena knew she could do it. She would have to if she wanted to find out how to get back home.

Gazing into the blue of the flame, orange and yellow dancing around the outside, red coals glowing on the edges of the burning wood became mesmerizing and soothing at the same time. It was easy to lose all thoughts and be empty, relaxed and blank. The sky was inky black in contrast. Looking up from the interior of the flames and across the fire-pit, Serena's eyes were met by the intense stare of golden yellow cougar eyes.

Other than the movement of her eyeballs, Serena remained calm and focused on slow deep breaths through her nostrils. She was already in a meditative state from staring into the depths of the fire and panicking at this point would be useless. The cougar sat there, bigger than life four feet from the opposite side of the fire, just staring at her.

Serena returned the glare and sat unmoving. Had it not been so unnerving to sit in the close proximity of a top predator, she might have noticed his perfectly smooth, clean, tawny coat and black tipped ears and tail. The tail, the end of it flicked with purpose and was only observed by her peripheral vision then she heard him. In her head, the gentle deep voice flowed like water over her brain.

"Pelipa, my sister, do not be afraid. I have come to assist you on your journey. You are a strong, good woman and have been chosen for a special purpose. I have come to tell you that there is a right time for everything. You will need to take action and you will need to rest, you must find the balance within yourself. You possess wise leadership but must wield that power well and not bask in its glory. Look deep within your heart, fight for what is right and never back down. This is your test, do not fail it or you will weep forever. The Creator will see you through. Heya."

A loud pop of the fire caused Serena to jerk to attention and with that the cougar was gone. Where was Rim? Serena looked frantically around to find Rim standing head low, sleeping by the trees. Blinking the vision from her eyes did nothing to dispel the message the Spirit had brought her this night. She really needed to turn in and get some rest. Dreamless sleep carried her on silent wings throughout the night and she slept in great peace.

The dark purple of night gave way to lavender hues as the sun made its way towards the eastern horizon. Serena opened her rested eyes to this stunning display of nature. Rim snorted nearby as the steam rose off the water to play in the light of the new day. It was calm and all was quiet in this heavenly place. Still quite cool, Serena extricated herself from the warmth of the buffalo robe. Something caused her to wake up, now she was ready to face it. A few sips of water from her canteen calmed her rumbling belly, only 24 hours to go.

Rim-Fyre walked over to stand beside her, nuzzling her hand as she gazed out over the steaming waters at the wonderment of daybreak. She turned to him and sensed that he wanted her to go with him. He nosed his side as if to say 'hop on, I'll take you there'. She jumped onto his back and in the semi-darkness Rim-Fyre took her to the place where they had loped to at liberty their first day out. He walked calmly to the rock pile where Serena dismounted and sat upon the rocks watching the new day come into being. Just as the first bright rays of sun filtered over the eastern hill, Serena sensed another presence and slowly turned to look behind her. There, hidden by the darkness was a small herd of buffalo shimmering to reality in the rays of the sun.

The enormous bull lifted his head as the sunlight touched him with her light and walked nearer to the rock pile where Serena sat. Rim-Fyre looked unaffected by this approach. She sat quietly and waited as the bull approached her with confidence. Serena was aware of the potential danger of an angered animal of his immense size but waited patiently until the lukewarm watery voice of the buffalo flowed into her head.

"Greetings, Sister Pelipa. Our days of great numbers are over but we will remain in spirit here in the grass. You must renew your connection to the Great Spirit through prayer and thankfulness. Be not ungrateful because you think you don't have what you want or need. Your reconnection will attract the good back into your life. You have great courage and strength within you to accept any challenge that comes to you, and abundance will come with knowledge. Go now to meet your destiny and remember the wise words of those that help you along the way. Heya."

Serena turned to observe Rim-Fyre on both knees bowing his head to the buffalo. The enormous bull nodded his head in their direction then turned westward to join his herd only to dissipate into the grass like smoke on the wind. Rim unfolded his front limbs and stood erect again as the sun now shone on them from high ahead. Serena stood on a rock at the edge of the pile and Rim-Fyre walked beside it to allow her easy access to his back. They walked together into the east and back toward the little camp.

After she drank her fill of water Serena went in the tent and fell fast asleep. She was exhausted from all of this talking with animal spirits. None of which had mentioned anything about what she would have to do to get home and when.

The sound of great flapping wings woke her from her nap. Serena became aware that her utmost attention was warranted. She scrambled from beneath the shade of the tent. The azure blue sky provided the perfect backdrop for the eagle perched on the only large branch sticking out from the birch tree, bathed in perfectly hued shades of orange and yellow. The bald eagle stood out in dark contrast with his nearly black body and daisy white head and tail.

Serena remained on her knees, as she gazed up at the very real eagle sitting there revered like a god. The voice was low and authoritative, "How are you feeling today daughter of mine?"

'In awe and wonderment,' she answered with her thoughts.

"Good!" the Spirit Eagle answered. "Listen carefully, the animal spirits that best represent you have come bearing messages to bring you closer to the Great Spirit and help you understand what is to come. We are but messengers between the here-and-now and the Great

One. Your future holds things that you will understand in time but first you must be open to them. If you close your mind to the possibilities you will not fulfill your destiny and that of your family. You must go home to your time and place but for that to happen, you must follow my guidance.

The ancient stones on the ground are magical. For them to work again you must place four stones between each of the stones present. Only four stones must be placed each day beginning on the new moon. In order for the portal to work, it must take you fourteen settings of the sun to complete. You must sing your own heart song while you place the stones, singing your spirit into the portal. It must be 'your' heart song, and no song that comes from your heart is wrong. The stones must be placed as the sun sets in the west. When you have completed placing the stones, the earth will turn one cycle. Upon the rising of the full moon you can ride into the ancient wheel and go home. It will only open for a few minutes and only you and your Spirit Guide may pass."

'Rim-Fyre?' she asked.

"Yes, he is your personal messenger, you cannot go without him. One last thing you must do. You must prepare and bestow a gift upon the brave Nawat Sinopa, he is troubled. You must gather bark from this tree to represent loyalty and spiritual growth, sage from the land for balance and purity, a feather from my breast for trust, honor and wisdom. These items must be bound together with the hair from your horse to include a small bit of his spiritual medicine. This is a friendship bundle. You will know when it's the right time to present it to him. May the Spirit be with you always. Heya."

Three small eagle breast feathers floated softly to the ground with the eagle's departure. Serena gathered them gently and held them close to her nose smelling their energy as the eagle wing feather thrummed in her shirt.

The breeze rustled the leaves on the trees and some of them fluttered to the earth, their season over. Serena tucked the nearly three inch long feathers into her shirt pocket as she stood up to examine the bark on the trees. Her knife was required to make a slice into the papery bark of the birch tree. Soon she had cut a piece approximately two inches by three. A short walk produced a few stems of fragrant sage, now all that was needed was some of Rim-Fyre's tail hairs.

Grazing a short distance away, Serena walked over to him, admiring how his short back joined the powerful hip. She reached out for his tail as she walked around him. He took no notice of the fact that she was cutting some of his hair as he grazed. The prairie grass invited her to take a seat a few feet away from Rim-Fyre. Within a few minutes she had fashioned a thin braid of about sixteen inches in length from Rim's luxurious hair. She glanced up and was confident that the small swatch of hair she cut would not be missed from his long, full flaxen tail. She had chosen reddish tail hair to compliment the colors of the friendship bundle. First she turned the bark of the birch tree so that it curved upward and she laid the sprigs of sage within the bark then gently placed the feather on top of the sage in a neat little bundle. She was able to wrap the length of braided horse hair around the bundle twice before tying it off neatly. She tucked the small prize in her shirt pocket for just the right moment to give it to Nawat Sinopa.

Rim came to lay as close as possible to Serena with his back to her, careful not to hit her with his hooves, then he stretched his neck out and rested his head on her lap. Serena shifted to accommodate him. "You know you're not a lap-dog, right?" she said stroking the side of his muzzle with her fingertips. He blew gently, fluttering his nostrils without spraying snot all over her. Serena smiled, "You're right, I need a nap too." Lying down on her back, she rested her head on open palms, closed her eyes and took in a cleansing breath.

Hearing yet another voice, she recognized in an instant that it was Rim. She was too tired to open her eyes so she listened to his sweet masculine voice. "Pelipa my sister, you and I have far to go, this journey is only the beginning. Search deep within yourself and gather the power within you to go forward and join me in the future. I will remain ever your guardian as long as I physically can. I would die for you. We will run together farther than far to fulfill our destiny. Eat and rest, there is much work to be done and then we will go home. Heya."

Serena opened her eyes, it was near sunset, the air was cooling already. "Rim, did you just talk to me?" But he was already up grazing two horse lengths away. A rumbling stomach reminded Serena that she had not eaten for three days. Initially she had planned on waiting until the fourth morning to break her fast but she was becoming weak and knew that she should eat a little bit tonight or she might be really sick tomorrow. With knowledge came the desire to continue on and do what she must in order to get home and she was going to need her strength for that.

    She gathered up enough wood to make a cheery little fire. Her supper consisted of bread and cheese which went amazingly well with a fresh cup of fire brewed coffee. Serena gave thanks to the Great Spirit for the food and was intensely grateful for her Spirit Helpers. It was dark by the time she was done eating, Rim took up his post nearby the trees and stood guard. A few more thick pieces of wood were added to the fire as the cool night air descended over the land. A restful sleep enveloped her in the warmth of the thrumming buffalo robe.

SIXTEEN
Thanksgiving and a Job

Saying thank you is more than good manners.
It's good spirituality.
~ Alfred Painter

From the top of the hill near the Knight property it looked like piles of snow off in the distance near the C.P.R. Roundhouse. Serena didn't recall seeing it there before and knew that it wasn't snow. It was another sunny morning and Mrs. Knight waved to her as she rode by.

Skirting her way around the Métis encampment she made her way directly to the C.P.R. Dining Hall which was situated north and west of the Roundhouse and water tank. Oxcarts with scrawny oxen driven by Métis were loaded with bones and made their way down the street to the piles on the north side of the tracks by the Roundhouse. It suddenly dawned on Serena that the piles of white she saw were mounds of buffalo bones.

This realization made her stomach feel queasy. So many hundreds of thousands of buffalo were mercilessly slaughtered here on the prairies. It was already done, only a few thousand might still remain on the land now, there was nothing she could do to change that.

Swift Current seemed to be busy this Saturday morning before Thanksgiving. At least five or six men rode by on horseback and a couple of oxcarts were making their way through town. Serena tucked Rim into the safety of the barn in case someone tried to steal him, not that that was likely to happen. Rim might have something to say about that.

Her horse now secured in the barn, Serena made her way to the Dining Room where saddled horses were tethered to the hitching rail outside. Several men sat at the tables in the room when she entered the north door. Joan waved a greeting as she poured coffee into mugs when Serena came in with her saddlebags slung over one arm.

"Morning, Miss Joan. How are you today?" She said tipping her hat.

"I'm well, Derek. I'll finish up here and meet you in the kitchen." Joan replied using her pseudonym.

Serena overheard Joan say to the men that she was her cousin visiting from back east. A short while later both women were in the kitchen discussing the plans for the Thanksgiving weekend. Over coffee and a fried egg sandwich Serena learned that a train was coming into town sometime today, possibly near noon. Freight had to be unloaded and loaded, four carloads of bones were going out and they all had to be pitched by hand. Joan warned Serena that Mac would more than likely recruit her to assist in unloading and reloading the train cars. A church service was going to be held at the Dining Hall the following day where members of the tiny community would bring food to be shared for the Thanksgiving meal following the service. Serena learned that the C.P.R. Dining Hall served as restaurant, hotel, meeting place, church and community hall. It would be a bustling and busy place for the next two days. She would have to step far out of her comfort zone to mingle with the locals, assist in loading train cars and socialize with the men, all while maintaining her farcical persona. Serena surmised that this might be her greatest challenge yet. Could she pull it off?

Joan had taken Katie over to one of the ladies in town to care for until Sunday, that way she could cook all day without interruption. A large batch of dough was in a bowl near the stove, warming and rising. The aroma of stew wafted throughout the kitchen. Lunch would be served early today so that everyone had eaten before the arrival of the train, which had to be unloaded and reloaded by nightfall.

Flour dusted the front of Joan's apron as she poured her yeast mixture into the flour in the dough bowl. "I just have to mix this up to rise so I can get my other dough into bread pans. I have just enough buns for lunch today. Both of these batches of bread are for tonight and tomorrow."

"That is a lot of work." Serena surmised. "No bakery in town here, eh?"

"Nope, not yet!" Joan chuckled. "I can hardly wait until someone comes into town and opens one. That will cut my workload in half."

"Is there anything I can do to help?" Serena asked. "I feel like I'm too dirty from camping out by the fire for the past three days. I'm sure I smell like a horse."

Joan laughed at that, "You smelling like horse sweat and smoke is a hundred times better than the body odor of all the men coming in to eat today. You just keep your odor. You'll fit right in working out there all afternoon. And be thankful for any breeze to blow everyone else's B.O. away. Mrs. Knight should be here soon to help with serving lunch today."

"Okay, what do you want me to do in the meantime?"

"Before we're disturbed and you're off to work for the whole afternoon, you can give me a brief rundown on your vision quest if you're so inclined to share it with me."

"… So now I suppose you think I'm a crazy, delusional maniac?" Serena said finishing up the condensed version of her experience.

Joan paused as she looked up from kneading her dough. "In some ways Serena, I envy you and wish I could go back to modern times and see my family. I miss them the most and I know that my mom and dad mourned for my loss." She stared at her dough for a moment, thinking, reflecting then looked at Serena again. "On the other hand I wouldn't have met Mac, who is the love of my life nor had Katie whom I love with all my heart. In answer to your question, no, I don't think you're crazy or delusional because I came through a time portal too. I came when Mac so obviously needed me. In my heart I'm sure I'm here for a really good reason, fulfilling my own destiny. I'm not sure exactly what that destiny is but I said before, maybe it's linked to being here for you. So that you can go back and fulfill yours."

Serena didn't have an opportunity to discuss it any further with Joan as the door chimed with entry and Mrs. Knight strode confidently into the kitchen.

"Morning, Joan, are we ready for this onslaught of men to feed? Oh! Good morning, Mr. Derek, I did not expect to see you here in Joan's kitchen."

"Sorry Agnes," Joan interjected. "I'd like you to meet my cousin from back east, Derek Tattum."

Mrs. Knight glanced at Joan. "Oh, we've met already. Perhaps he told you about grabbing a sandwich at my place in exchange for chores when he rode into town on that fancy stallion of his. I didn't realize he was your cousin, seeing as he didn't say anything about you when we met." Mrs. Knight's tone became extremely suspicious of the relationship between Joan and Derek. "Not that it's any of my business."

When Mrs. Knight walked to the stove and had her back to her, Serena gave a wide eyed expression and mouthed, 'what the hell?' to Joan. "I'll just head out now and see where Mac might need my help. See you at lunch, Joan. It was nice to meet you again, Mrs. Knight," Serena said placing her hat on her head as she walked around the corner and out into the dining room. *NOT!* She thought to herself, hoping that Mrs. Knight was not prone to gossip and would keep her suspicions to herself.

Finding herself in need of fresh air, Serena walked straight to the door and outside. Three men stood outside, deep in conversation. Serena wasn't sure if she should go to the barn and check on her horse or not.

She didn't want to appear unsociable knowing that lunch would be served in half hour.

"Excuse me," one of the men said to her. Serena committed him to memory. He was well dressed in a bowler hat, brown woolen overcoat and matching trousers. His fashionable dark moustache made him appear to be in his thirties. He continued, "I don't believe we've met before. Are you Miss Joan's cousin we've heard Mac talking about?"

Serena addressed him politely, "Why yes, sir, I am. The name's Derek Tattum." She held out her hand which he accepted, squeezing and pumping her hand with confidence.

"I'm John Thomas and these gentlemen are local merchants, Don Franklin and Mark Wilson." He released her hand and she shook hands with the other men who were also dressed in woolen coats and trousers of varying shades of brown. "Mac said you have a fancy stallion that you brought with you from the east. We heard he's got a hell of a neck and shoulder on him. Are we going to get to see this horse sometime? We're always in need of some new bloodlines in these parts here."

"Mr. Thomas, I will be in town here for the next few weeks anyway, I'm sure you'll get to see him." She smiled slightly.

"Well, me and the fellers here were just discussing a dilemma that's come up. One of our draft horses has come up lame and our one horse won't be able to pull the freight wagon alone. The wagon has to go from the train here to the 76 Ranch with winter supplies. Perhaps we could pay you something for the use of your horse, if you're up for the job. You interested?"

Serena felt confident in her reply, "My horse will pull. I've never had him hooked up before but that's what he was bred for. He's not real big but he's tough and he's got heart."

The merchant named Don chuckled, "I've never seen a saddle horse hitched with a draft before. Ol' Ben is 17.2 HH."

"After lunch then, Mr. Derek?" John asked baiting her.

"Sure, you bet." Serena tipped her hat to the men and excused herself to go to the barn and check on Rim. His familiar nicker greeted her as she walked in the open barn door. Hinged window flaps had been opened to allow airflow through the little building. She forked some hay into the manger for Rim to eat while she gathered brushes to smooth and shine his coat. His coat was fuzzier now in preparation for the coming winter.

"Rim, I got us a job after lunch. I hope you'll work with me. It's a job pulling in harness. It's way better than me pitching buffalo bones all afternoon when that train gets here. At least this way, we'll get to work together." Running her fingers through his thick mane, she detangled it hoping it wouldn't interfere with the harness. "There now, you look amazing." Rim blew three short bursts through his nostrils as he chewed on his hay. "I'll go have my lunch now and see you in a bit." She patted his hindquarters as she walked past him and out the door.

The Dining Room was fair bustling with merchants, cowboys, Métis and a few Indians as Serena sat down at one of the tables with Mac and some other men she assumed worked for the C.P.R. There didn't appear to be an empty table in the room which was filled with the sound of scraping chairs and a multitude of conversations going on all at once. By Serena's best estimate there were at least forty men assembled here today. Mrs. Knight came by to serve coffee. Joan carried in plates heaped with stew and a buttered bun for each of them.

"So I heard you and your horse got a job this afternoon, Derek." Mac said taking a bite of his bun.

Serena swallowed her mouthful of food before answering. "Word gets around fast. Yes, Mr. John Thomas and his associates appeared to be short a horse for their team. Apparently you did a great job of bragging up my horse." She said raising an eyebrow in question.

"Ah, that ain't nothin'. Your horse looks real powerful even though he's not very big. Good on you for getting a job though, now I don't have to ride your ass to pitch buffalo bones this afternoon." Mac and the other men at the table laughed at that remark. "Joanie said she'd given you the heads up already."

Giving him a wry smile and a nod of her head, she muttered, "Thanks."

Far in the distance a train whistle blew. The men in the room donned their hats, stood up and put money on the table. The sound of forty wooden chairs scraping on the floor followed by boot steps filled the room. The door-bell clanged every time someone bumped or moved the door on their way out. The whistle blew again, closer this time. When Serena made her way to and out the door she could hear the chugga-chugga of the steam engine coming down the track. To the east she could see the smoke rolling off the train engine stack as it released a hiss of steam and blew its whistle, twice, long and high pitched signifying its arrival. She hoped that the train racket wasn't bothering Rim too much. He'd never seen or heard a steam engine before and until now, she hadn't either.

John Thomas waited for Serena outside the Dining Room door. "Mister Derek, go fetch your horse and I'll ride with you to the stables where the wagon and other horse are. We'll hitch there."

"Alright, I'll be right back with him." Wading her way through the men receiving instructions for unloading the freight train, Serena made her way to the barn. The engine stopped east of where the barn and Dining Hall were located. The water tower was there and the train would require a fill. Rim seemed excited as she approached him with his bridle. Bridled, she led him from the dim light of the little barn to the full daylight outside. She mounted him bareback and rode around the men milling about on their way down the street to the train. Other wagons or carts pulled by oxen, teams or mules were already making their way to the train to procure their goods.

John Thomas sat on his bay saddle horse waiting for Serena to ride around the crowd. Rim-Fyre gathered himself proudly and jogged over to the bay gelding. Mr. John Thomas spurred his gelding forward, lurching as his horse jumped ahead to step in front of Rim to go down the main street. They rode to the back of the mercantile shop and their stables. Serena thought John rode like a sack of potatoes and felt sorry for the gelding. Rim kept up his proud jog as she sat unmoving on his bare back. From all appearances, Serena knew she had the most beautiful –fancy- horse there for miles and miles around.

A large Belgian cross gelding, without an ounce of fat on him, stood hooked to a large four wheel wagon in front of the stables. The wagon fit the horse and this was going to be Rim's team-mate. Ben, the Belgian, stood there asleep in his traces. John waved her over to the stable door where he dismounted and allowed his horse to walk in and find its own stall. They would find a harness to fit Rim before hooking him to the wagon.

A grizzled, grey haired man of about sixty, garbed in greasy clothing and an equally greasy bent out of shape hat with a hole in it followed them into the stable. John introduced him as Pete, their wagon driver. The entire front stall on the left side of the entry was filled with harnesses, saddles and other tack. Pete quickly looked over Rim and walked to a set of harness that he was sure would fit him. He spat brown tobacco juice at Serena's feet as he brought over the collar to fit around Rim's neck. Rim laid his ears back and backed away.

"Let me put it on him," Serena said holding out her hand. "Just tell me what to do."

"Right," Pete said, handing her the collar. "This is gonna be some hitch, le' me tell ya."

Serena placed the collar around Rim's neck and fastened it at his mane with the buckle. It fit well on his thick muscular neck and rested on the front of his shoulder. Next, Pete handed her the rest of the harness which was all hooked together; it included the girth, hames and traces and the breeching which went over the hindquarters of the horse. Rim stood quietly as long as Pete and John maintained a safe distance from him. Pete gave instructions on placing the hames over the collar and fastening that attached at the bottom of the collar by his chest. The girth, of course, was done up where a saddle girth went, the breeching over his rump and the crouper under his tail to hold the breeching in place. The traces went through a keeper on the breeching as well. The traces were placed over Rim's back to walk him over to the wagon and his mate until he was hooked up. Lastly, she was handed a headstall with blinders on it. Seeing as this was Rim's first time being hitched, Serena felt it was safer to use the blinders than his own bridle. After removal of his bridle Rim accepted the harness bridle without consequence. Long lines were then attached to the bit on the harness bridle. Pete told Serena to back Rim into position beside Ben. As if he had done it before, Rim backed readily into position beside the tongue of the wagon and Ben. The traces were hitched to the eveners and a snap was hitched onto the yoke in the front - this kept the horses moving together and held the end of the tongue of the wagon. Lastly the reins had to be sorted, Rim was on the right side so a short rein connected the horses to each other, only the outside rein was used to turn both horses at the same time because the horses were hitched together by the inside rein.

John shook his head as he eyed the unlikely team with great speculation and Pete swore a stream knowing he was going to be the laughing stock of town. Serena had to admit that Rim and Ben looked downright ridiculous. Rim looked like a pony beside Ben, his abundant mane and forelock made him appear even more pony-like. There was nearly a foot in height difference and more than 500 pounds separated the two. Rim was only two-thirds the size of Ben.

Pete explained to Derek/Serena that when they stopped, he was going to be the horse handler. Hold the horses while the rest of them loaded and or unloaded the wagon and to be prepared for an onslaught of ridicule.

Before climbing into the wagon with Pete, Serena stood before Rim-Fyre bridle cheek pieces in hand. "Alright Rim, let's do this. We are not going to be the laughing stock. You are a proud Canadian and don't you forget it!" She winked at him because she knew Pete was watching and she couldn't give him a kiss on the nose like she wanted to.

Pete slapped the rein on Ben's hindquarters; Rim-Fyre's rump was too far below his rein to reach. Ben stepped into the collar and Rim walked forward with him stepping out evenly into the collar like any good teammate would. Thus far the wagon was empty and the pulling was easy. Rim walked evenly with Ben around each of the turns to go down the street to the railcars where they would load the freight going to the 76 Ranch.

Bystanders pointed and laughed as they came down the street to take their place at the railcar to load. Several carts and wagons were already loaded and pulling away from the train with their cargo. There were lots of derogatory comments of "nice team" and "cute pony" as they made their way to the train.

As instructed, Serena jumped down and held the team while John found some help to load their wagon.

John barked instructions for where to load what sacks or supplies on the wagon while Pete packed the back to get the most out of the space on the farm wagon. It took nearly an hour to load and it was heaped as high as it could be when they were done. The wagon rocked a little even with the brake on as the men loaded who knows what on the back of it. Serena was sure she had seen a ton of iron pieces of some description get packed on there. The wagon groaned with the weight of it.

"Alright lackey, jump on the wagon, we got four miles to go to the Ranch!" Pete yelled at her. John rode his saddle horse beside the wagon, he would be making the trip to unload at the 76 Ranch and receive payment for the merchandise he'd sold.

"Yaaa!" Pete shouted as he laid the reins to Ben. Both horses leaned into their collars, the big Belgian and the little Canadian. Ben was really leaning forward and pushing with his hind feet in the dirt but the wagon didn't budge. Serena watched Rim-Fyre lean into the collar and squat down then jumped forward in the traces. The wagon rolled a little, once momentum was achieved, both horses continued moving forward.

"Well I'll be," Pete said. "Never seen a horse squat down and jump in the traces like that little feller. It's like he knew what he was doin'."

Serena didn't let Pete see her smile. She was quietly proud of Rim. It was tough going with a couple tons of merchandise on the wagon, not to mention really bumpy. Four miles may as well have been forty. The trail took them through a coulee to skirt around a big hill. It was an hour pull out to the 76 Ranch north of town along the Battleford Trail. So named because it was the route taken to the Battlefords where the Riel Rebellion had taken place and was still being used to go there.

A few times Pete had to get after Ben for allowing Rim-Fyre to pull ahead and pull more than his fair share of the weight. By now it was mid-afternoon, ranch hands came out to greet them. They pulled the wagon up to the barn. Serena held the team and Pete brought them water while the ranch hands unloaded the wagon. Ben was soaking wet with sweat whereas Rim-Fyre was just warm and showing a little sweat under the collar. Serena was glad they rode all those miles out to the Cypress Hills and back a week ago. It whipped Rim-Fyre into grand physical condition.

Pete smiled his nearly toothless grin at Serena, "That's a fine wee hoss you have there, lad. I'd hitch him to my wagon any day."

Serena managed a "thank you," as she gently stroked Rim and told him what a good boy he was.

Some of the ranch hands guffawed at the size difference of the team but were swiftly reprimanded by both John and Pete. The little Canadian horse had made an impression.

The horses jingled right along on the way back to town with an empty wagon. Rim-Fyre was still fresh and interested in going forward while Ben pulled back in the traces not quite up to the pace Rim wanted to jog.

"That's our load for the day," John announced, speaking to Serena. "I have to admit I'm impressed with your little horse. He is tough as nails. Would you be interested in hitching him with Ben twice a week to haul out to the ranches when the trains come in with supplies? I could pay you $2.00 a load. Maybe in a couple weeks, Ben's team-mate will be sound."

Wow, last of the big time spenders. Serena thought. *But then again, who knows what the going rate is.* "Is that the going rate?" she asked him.

"Well I would offer to buy your horse for $150 but I'm pretty sure you're not going to part with him. Plus he seems awful fond of you."

"You're right, he's not for sale. I could use some spending money while I'm here visiting my cousin. So sure, we'll do it, for a couple weeks anyway."

They unhitched the horses and John paid Serena $2.00 for the load. She hopped on Rim and loped off down the street towards the barn. It was late afternoon but Rim was rubbed down and fed for the night. Serena walked down the street toward the workers loading buffalo bones on the rail cars. Two rail cars were heaping full of buffalo bones and there was still an enormous pile left to load.

Mac split the men into two groups to load both rail cars simultaneously. With only a few hours of daylight left, Mac was in a hurry to get the train loaded before dark. They were all tired and hungry but there would be no supper until the train was ready to roll out.

Serena pitched right in beside Mac and threw the bones on the train car. It was sad to think of the thousands of buffalo that had been slaughtered for their bones to be carted off somewhere to be ground into fertilizer.

The pile of bones began to dwindle as they picked up the last of them and tossed them on the rail car.

Mac dismissed some of the men and sent them to the Dining Room to eat. Serena stayed and helped to toss the last ones up. The train conductor spoke with Mac for a few minutes more then climbed onto the engine and revved it up.

"A job well-done, Derek." Mac offered. "I don't know about you but I'm starving. Let's go eat."

The train whistle blew twice to signify its departure as they walked into the dining room which was full again with all the men helping. Serena noticed two more women helping Joan with serving the men that came in for supper. Mac and Serena washed up in the rain barrel outside so at least their hands and faces were clean.

The camaraderie in the room was evident. Several of the men came over and slapped Serena on the back, "well done, lad. That's some little horse you got yourself. Glad to see he can pull his weight. He works harder than the big horse. Well worth his weight in gold" were, just some of the compliments heaped on her this evening. Serena just smiled and nodded her acceptance while trying to eat and enjoy her meal of roast mutton, potatoes and beets. The homemade slice of bread was the best part of the meal.

A handful of men including John, Pete, Don and Mark pulled chairs up to their table to chit chat over drinks after the meal. Mac procured a barrel of ale and everyone that worked today was privy to a mug.

"So tell us more about this little horse of yours, Derek," Don prompted. "Where'd he come from exactly?"

"Well, I bought this stallion in Quebec from a farmer there as I was passing through. Where exactly is irrelevant, the point is, there are a few more of this type of horse in Quebec than there are out west here."

"So he's a little French horse?" Mark asked. "Did it take him long to learn English?"

Everyone burst out laughing at Mark's question. "Yeah, yeah," they wanted to know, "could he only speak French?"

Serena shook her head and suppressed an outright laugh at their silliness. "Well, it just so happens that I know universal horse language so we got along well from the start." Heads nodded in acknowledgement. "I did learn more about the breed, though. The French call them le Cheval Canadien which is the Canadian Horse. This Canadian is a descendant of the horses that King Louis the XIV sent over to the French Colonies in the late 1600's. They were typical of the horses bred in France at that time." The men were thoroughly engrossed in her story so she went on. "The breed remained pure and free of crossbreeding for over 150 years, separated by the Appalachian mountain range and the fact that the French and English were at war with one another." She paused.

"Go on," John prompted.

"The French nobility used the Canadian horse as their work horse, their Sunday cart horse and riding horse; they were basically used for everything. The horses proved to be tough and hardy in this wild and untamed land. We know all about that, right?" She asked.

"Here, here," they all chimed in and clinked their mugs as they took another swallow of ale.

"The farmer said that the Americans bought many of the Canadian horses and took them to the States as remounts and artillery horses during the Civil War because they were tougher and calmer than most other breeds of horses. He was reluctant to sell me this young stallion but I offered him a good dollar and he liked the way the horse and I bonded, so couldn't refuse. Then I brought this Canadian horse out west with me when I came to visit my cousin Joan." Serena finished up her story. She was exhausted and didn't want to be the center of attention anymore.

Joan came into the dining room to speak with Mac for a few minutes and left.

"Alright guys, it's time we pack it in. Tomorrow is Thanksgiving and my wife wants to tidy up before church in the morning. I hope you plan on coming back for church and dinner tomorrow." Mac announced.

Most of the men sitting around the table had homes to go to so they shook hands with Mac and Serena and went home.

Mrs. Knight and the other ladies had left to go home already so clean-up was left to Joan in preparation for tomorrow. Mac and Serena helped by moving tables and chairs around while Joan wiped off the tables and gave the floor a good sweeping.

"I have a pot of tea on in the kitchen and water boiling for a wash. It's getting late so no proper bath today. Sorry."

They each got a bucket of warm water, a piece of soap and a rough cotton towel to wash up with. Serena carried her bucket upstairs to her room with her to wash up in privacy and go straight to bed. Tomorrow would be another busy, social day.

Serena marveled at Joan's ability to find clothing for her that would hide her womanly curves, not that they were that obvious with her trim athletic build. A beige cotton button shirt, one size big, a button vest in a brown and canvas pants –jeans- two sizes too big, was left for her on the chair for the next day. Serena had to use her own belt and was glad she wore one the day she left home. She let her hair fall where it may and ran her fingers through it, hoping that would suffice for Thanksgiving celebrations.

A cup of coffee to start the day, even Mac was down in the kitchen this fine Sunday morning. "I fed the horses already. Your stallion was happy to take a drink of water from my bucket this morning without trying to take my ear off." He chuckled at that. "Have your coffee and then give me a hand moving tables, we're having serve-yourself breakfast for the guests staying here. Then we gotta get ready for church service and dinner after."

"No problem," Serena replied.

The tables in the dining area were set end to end with the chairs on either side for breakfast. Mac and Serena helped Joan carry out the large dishes of French toast and ham. Guests came down, filled their plates and then piled the empties back up on the side table when they were finished eating. The honor system was in place this morning for breakfast, a jar was left at the end of the table for payment. Joan served coffee then breakfast was over and cleaned up within an hour. Serena helped Joan wash dishes while Mac and the other men moved the tables to the side and set the chairs for church.

The locals filtered into the C.P.R. Dining Room for church, approximately 50 people with the workers showed up for the Thanksgiving service. Pastor David Beckett gave a wonderful sermon on gratefulness for what a person already had and thanksgiving of course.

Serena was deep in her own thoughts about gratefulness and giving thanks for what she had, while the Pastor spoke about the Heavenly Father and what his plans were for his flock. As he spoke, the memories of the Spirit Eagle's visit came to mind. The Eagle reminded her to rekindle her relationship with the Creator and be grateful for what she had. By doing just that, it would open up the world to her, to receive so much more. The pastor seemed to be saying the same thing, only he was using different words. – Amen.

With the church service over, everyone said a bunch of "God Bless you, Good Morning, Happy Thanksgiving" and so on, exchanging pleasantries. Tables and chairs were moved again while the local guests went to get their contribution to the Thanksgiving meal and several other town folk who missed church came in bearing hot pans of food for the potluck meal. The Dining Room was fairly buzzing with activity and for the first time, Serena noticed children of the people who lived here. She wondered where they had been hiding. There were boys and girls of varying ages, about a dozen of them.

Once the food had been laid out on the tables and everyone exchanged greetings, Mac stood on a chair and hollered to get everyone to quiet down so Pastor Beckett could say a prayer over the meal.

There was so much food and a wide variety of everything to eat. Serena made a point of eating hearty.

The pumpkin pie was her favorite part of the meal complete with a healthy dollop of heavy cream on it. Somewhere, someone here had a milk cow. There was much back slapping and congratulations on showing everyone what a grand and powerful little horse her stallion was. Serena almost choked a few times for back slaps while she had a mouthful of food.

Everyone assisted with clean-up when the meal was over. Serena assisted the men in moving tables and carrying out clean pots and roasting pans to the neighbor's carriages or buckboards. Here, too, the townsfolk with women and children used their saddle horses for driving as well as riding.

Most of the neighbors were gone by mid-afternoon and Serena was able to sneak out to the barn and ride Rim-Fyre bareback. Almost everyone she saw on the way waved to her as she made her way over the railroad tracks and down toward the creek. It was nice to find a fairly quiet place to relax and watch the water ripple and glint in the sunlight with her favorite horse.

SEVENTEEN

Magic Stones

Magic is believing in yourself, if you can do that, you can do anything.
~ Johann Wolfgang von Goethe

It snowed a few days after Thanksgiving. Pete advised Serena to put shoes with studs on Rim-Fyre or he wouldn't have the traction he needed to pull a load on the slick surface. She relented because she couldn't risk Rim getting injured even though he'd never had a set of shoes on in his life.

The two trips they made that week were long and cold. Between the snow and barely freezing temperatures, travel was treacherous and made pulling hard for both Rim and Ben. Even though it wasn't snowing on Wednesday, it took hours for Serena to thaw out after the day's travels. Rim showed no indication of being anything less than fine.

When the train rolled in to town on Saturday, it was snowing. Rim and Ben were hitched and loaded. Their delivery was to a ranch 8 miles northeast of town. John Thomas rode with them on each of the merchandise deliveries. Serena wasn't sure if it was because he didn't trust Pete to get the load there or if it was a lack of trust in receiving payment. There was a large hill to traverse on their way to the ranch north of town. Even with studded shoes on the horses it was hard pulling up the hill. Ben slipped and went down on his knees smashing his tender nose into the ground. The Belgian's lip got cut on his teeth and sprayed blood in the snow when he snorted. Pete was sure Ben broke his nasal bone and his right knee began to swell. They were two thirds of the way up the hill and on a level spot so didn't have to concern themselves with losing the wagon down the hill. There were two miles left to go.

If Pete was anything, he was a caring horseman. John protested as Pete unhooked Ben from the wagon. "If we're going to save this horse to use him this winter, you will have to take him back to the stable Mister Thomas." He handed Ben's lines over to John while he sat on his horse. "Walk him slow."

John reluctantly handed the merchandise invoice to Serena, "Don't let Mr. Decker talk his way out of paying. I need full payment for this invoice. Now that's a lot of money I'm trusting you with. Don't let me down." The look he gave her was one of 'if you don't come back, I'll find you and kill you.'

"Yes sir, Mr. Thomas." Serena answered confidently.

Now that Ben was unhooked, the tongue of the wagon and yoke were removed. One of the eveners was taken off and the other one was hooked up in the center of the wagon. Rim would have to pull the load by himself. The only problem was that with the tongue removed, the wagon could hit him. The horse couldn't control the speed of the wagon without the tongue and yoke, Pete would have to ride the park brake down the slopes.

The powerful hindquarters bunched as the dark chestnut stallion crouched down while leaning into the collar of the harness. A well sprung leap forward was able to get the wagon rolling. Rim continued slowly up the incline placing his hooves wide and sure. Serena walked beside him the rest of the way up the hill. From this vantage point they were able to see the ranch buildings to the east, another mile on more level terrain would see them to the ranch. Looking back, Serena could see John making his way across the bottom of the large valley with the Belgian in tow.

Steaming with sweat when they pulled the wagon in front of the barn, Rim-Fyre stood quietly as the ranch hands began to unload the wagon. Huge snowflakes continued their downward spiral in the calm, gloom of the afternoon. Serena located a woolen rug in the back of the wagon and tossed it over Rim's wet back and neck to wick away some of the moisture and prevent him from getting a chill. If his muscles got cold, he wouldn't be able to work and pull the empty wagon back to town.

Mr. Decker introduced himself and invited Derek/Serena into the house to settle up the invoice. A brief explanation of why Mr. Thomas did not accompany them on the trip resolved any misgivings Mr. Decker had about paying Derek for his load of merchandise. The entire load of merchandise was $147.00 which Mr. Decker paid out in smaller bills including more than twenty one dollar bills. Serena refrained from saying anything but she hadn't seen one dollar bills for a long time. She marked the bill paid, wadded up the cash and stuck it in her shirt pocket. They shook hands and Serena returned to her horse.

As the afternoon wore on, Pete felt it best to leave the woolen rug on Rim-Fyre for the return trip. The wagon was empty now and much easier to pull. After a drink of water and nearly an hour rest, Rim was raring to go. With Serena and Pete in the wagon he jogged the first mile until they started their way down the long hill into the valley. Serena jumped off the wagon and walked with Rim down the hill, calming him just in case the wagon bumped him in the hocks. Pete was an excellent driver and he tied the reins up and rode the brakes hard all the way down the hill. Serena slipped a few times on the snow slick grass but caught herself on Rim's harness before she hit the ground.

Smoke came off the hot leather brake pads on the steepest parts of the decline as Pete held them with all his might. A few times he even shouted at Derek/Serena to walk the horse faster so the wagon wouldn't hit him. Rim-Fyre wanted to go crosswise on the hill, making large long zig-zags. This worked well on the steepest parts but took an hour to reach the bottom of the valley and onto the flat.

The cloud cover and gloom of the snowfall made it appear as if night were approaching. It was four more miles to the stables. Even though Serena was walking, her feet were frozen from walking in wet boots. Climbing back in the wagon, Pete took up the reins again and asked Rim to jog for most of the way back to town. Serena jumped off the wagon and walked the last stretch with her horse, so happy to see the buildings ahead.

Once back at the snug little barn at the C.P.R. Dining Room Rim got an extra measure of hay and a good rub down with an old rag. Serena found a woolen rug to place over Rim-Fyre for the night. She hugged him and went in to tend to her own needs and thaw out, her feet hurting with every step.

A corn broom was propped up against the entry of the Dining Hall so Serena used it to sweep the snow off the step and her boots before she walked in. Men were eating in the dining room when Serena walked through the doors, they glanced up and a few waved their acknowledgement. She entered the kitchen to warm up at the stove while Joan bustled about.

"You look frozen. Best get those boots and coats off so you can dry them. I'll fix a plate and leave it on the butcher block for you. Help yourself to some coffee while I finish cleaning up dirty plates." Joan said rushing off into the other room.

Serena sat with her stocking feet propped up on a foot stool near the stove, eating her supper while soaking up the radiant heat coming off the kitchen implement. Her cheeks and feet were burning from thawing, it was almost unbearable. Rubbing her feet together some helped ease the sensation.

Joan walked in as Serena placed the last forkful of potatoes in her mouth. "Alright now, dishes and sweep up in the other room and then a bath. You up for a bath Serena?"

"A bath, I can have a bath? No joke?"

"No Joke! Katie is at Helena's until tomorrow morning. Mac is gone to the Wilson's for at least two or three hours. And, I'm going to close and lock this kitchen door when the last customer leaves so that you and I can have a bath. Not together of course, but none-the-less ... a bath!" Joan smiled widely.

Serena was beginning to thaw enough now that it didn't feel like she was walking on pins and needles anymore. She dried dishes and put them away while Joan washed them. Large pots of water covered the entire surface of the kitchen stove to boil water for a bath. Joan had a large wooden tub that could be filled, enough water to soak in and bathe. A moveable screen was set up around the tub in the corner to allow for a modicum of privacy. Joan would quickly bathe first and then allow Serena to soak while Joan dried her long hair at the stove and visited with her from behind the screen.

Serena enjoyed each of the fifteen minutes she spent languishing in the hot scummy water of the bath, quickly washing her hair and body first and then just soaking up what heat was left in the water. It felt like heaven to her and for the first time in weeks she felt clean and refreshed. The warm bath relaxed her so much that she nearly fell asleep. Joan had to finally wake her and make her dry off so that they could pail the water out.

Dressed in fresh clean clothes, the women enjoyed a final cup of tea after their baths and retired for the evening. Serena wasted no time in crawling into bed and falling fast asleep.

Keeping track of the days and the change of moon, Serena realized that the new moon was that following Monday. With the change of moon came a lull in the weather and nicer days. The sun was back in all its shining glory and began to melt the three inches of snow that had fallen the previous week. This made mud but the warmth was worth it.

After each meal served at the Dining Hall, Serena scraped up the mud and cleaned floors. Serena had given fair warning to Joan that she would be away every afternoon and back at dark. She would have to be at the Medicine Wheel during sunset.

Horse and rider loped over the southern-most hill near the C.P.R. outpost known as Swift Current. They carefully walked down the slush covered slope into the valley in the late afternoon sun. It was nearly five miles to the sacred place where they were going. Loping on the flats and where the footing was good, Serena and Rim-Fyre rode to the Medicine Wheel in under an hour.

Serena dismounted, tied the reins around Rim's neck allowing him to graze while she put her energy into the task at hand. Four stones were required to be placed every day as the sun was setting, placed while singing her heart song. She was glad that she had pulled most of the grass around the stones when she was here little more than a week ago. Marveling at how things looked differently with some snow still on the ground. She had a little time yet before the sun would set to find stones suitable to place into the circle. Wandering some distance from the stone circle to find four stones, most of which fit nicely in her hand, except one was larger and weighed about seven pounds. It begged to be picked up. *How was that possible?*

The stones were carried to the wheel. It wasn't time yet to place them and Serena had no idea what her heart song was. The stone formation required some study before the sun was ready to set. The woman pretending to be a man, standing there with her prize chestnut stallion grazing, removed her hat and bent her head to pray. "God, Creator, Great Spirit, whatever you are, my heart is heavy and I've been given instructions I don't understand. I will do whatever it takes to get home to my family, in my time. They need me as much as I need them. I'm sorry for drifting away from you and not being grateful for the things that made up the life that I love. If there is a greater purpose for me, I pray that it will reveal itself so that I might take action and be a service to you and all of creation. Please bring the song that's in my heart to my mind so that I might sing my spirit into these stones. Guide my hands and my heart to your purpose so that I can serve you well. Thank you for all you do. Amen – Heya."

The sun appeared to sit on the edge of the horizon waiting for Serena to sing her stones into place. Again she took in the entire formation, the path and the circle, the opening to the south or almost south. Thoughts of a clock came to mind, where should she place the first set of stones on the day of the new moon? It came to her through the thought process: begin at the left hand side of the path and place the stones clockwise. The sun dipped lower and began to go behind the horizon. An old John Denver tune that she heard as a little girl came to mind. The song was Country Roads. Why that song? The words were wrong so she would have to make something up. With the first stone in hand at the ready she began to sing to the tune of Country Roads, "Magic stones take me home, to the place I belong. South Saskatchewan, Prairie Father, take me home magic stones." One stone was held reverently as she sang and then placed beside the first stone on the left hand side of the pathway. With second stone in hand she sang on, "I hear his voice, in the evening hour he calls me. My horse reminds me of my home far away. Listening to the Spirits and placing stones here, I get the feeling that in the moonlight I may go home." The second stone was placed and the third was placed as she sang her chorus again. She couldn't think of a second verse so she sang the chorus for the fourth and final stone she placed. The sun winked out on the horizon as she finished her song leaving a glowing orange and purple sunset.

The air grew colder with the setting sun. The snow making the air feel quite cold so Serena did not waste any time in riding her horse back to Joan's. Darkness would be evident as they arrived back at the little barn that was beginning to feel like a home away from home.

Sunny days were the norm for the remainder of the week. It was fortuitous and made hauling freight for John Thomas more efficient on Wednesday. Ben was still sore but had healed under Pete's great care enough to be hitched with Rim-Fyre. They were back at the stable by four in the afternoon which gave Serena sufficient time to ride out and sing her four stones into place in the Medicine Wheel.

She lingered at the stones after she placed them, it was significant somehow. The placement of stones was now complete on the first section of the circle. Rim-Fyre stood close to her while she pondered if there were forces far greater than herself at work here. *How did it all fit together and what was its purpose?* 'Do you have faith?' popped into her head. "Now where did that come from?" she asked aloud. She looked the stallion right in the eye and asked him, "Are these thoughts in my head coming from you?" He returned her hard stare with his liquid soft eye and blinked. "I wonder sometimes. Am I crazy, delusional, a freak? I've talked to Spirit Animals or are they real? I can't tell. Maybe being here isn't real either." 'Oh, it's real.' *Another answered thought in her head. Thought? Or voice?* Serena sat down on one of the larger stones, "I have faith. If I didn't, I wouldn't be following through on the advice from all the Spirit Helpers and I wouldn't be placing these stones hoping and praying that by doing this we will go home on the full moon. Now let's go back to the Dining Room and get some rest. It's been a long day and I'm tired."

'I'm tired, too, let's go.' Serena eyed Rim-Fyre with great speculation while she placed her foot in the stirrup. He seemed to look at her as if to say, 'hurry up.'

Serena and Rim continued their daily ritual of trekking out to the Medicine Wheel before sunset so Serena could sing her spirit into the stones and place them into the stone formation.

Saturday was another work day for Rim to be hitched with Ben. The weather continued its milder temperatures. The train wasn't in until after 2 o'clock that afternoon and by the time they returned to Swift Current, the sun was making a rapid descent to the western horizon. There was no time to stop for a saddle today. Serena rode straight out of the merchant stables bareback at a hard gallop and pushed Rim-Fyre all the way south to the sacred grounds. Not only did Rim-Fyre pull a wagon load of merchandise six miles twice, now Serena was asking him to run flat out for another four and a half. She stretched forward on his neck and gripped with her knees as they streaked across the countryside.

Serena was able to find four stones quite quickly as if they were waiting there for her to find them. She took several deep breaths to calm herself after their frantic speedy ride so that she could sing the stones into place. The sun winked its departure behind the western horizon as she sang the last stone into place. "Magic stones take me home to the place I belong, South Saskatchewan Prairie Father, take me home magic stones."

Movement caught her eye when Rim nickered a greeting to Nawat Sinopa's Appaloosa mare as they rode toward them in the sunsets orange glow. Serena's heart skipped a beat and she felt anxious but happy to see him for the first time in two weeks. Perhaps it was the physical attraction to him that kept her from visiting him. She was married to a man who she loved dearly and there was no point in placing herself in temptation's way. Inhaling a cleansing breath, Serena willed herself to other thoughts. She might be able to control herself but what of Nawat Sinopa? On their journey to visit his uncle, he looked at her with something akin to desire which she had blatantly ignored.

As Nawat Sinopa and his mare approached, he greeted her warmly. "Hello, Serena. I saw you race by on the wings of an eagle."

Serena couldn't suppress the smile that came naturally, "Hello, Nawat Sinopa. It is good to see you. Yes, Rim-Fyre can fly when he sets his mind to it." She patted Rim's neck as he stood close to her.

Nawat Sinopa recognized the body language of the red stallion as he stood like a stallion would to protect his mares. No one was touching her as long as he was around. "Would you ride with me?" He asked.

"Of course. How's the knee and ribs?" She asked as she leapt on Rim bareback.

"Much better. I felt like an old woman for over a week, resting and taking tea all the time but it healed well." He chuckled at that.

His smile and laughter made her stomach feel weird. What was wrong with her? She was feeling like a lovestruck teenager. She reminded herself that she was married and had a destiny to fulfill which was not here in this time and place.

"Can you even go back to your home?" He asked as they rode side by side down the creek to the place where the water was low and they could cross to the other side.

"That is the plan, yes, on the Hunter's Moon."

"It is good," Nawat Sinopa said softy.

They rode together quietly as the inky darkness made its way westward across the sky, both lost in their own thoughts. They parted at the bottom of the hill and promised they would see each other again before Serena went home on the full moon.

EIGHTEEN
Commitment

Flaming enthusiasm, backed up by horse sense and persistence, is the quality that most frequently makes for success.
~ Dale Carnegie

As each day came to a close, Serena would ride Rim-Fyre nearly five miles south of the little town and C.P.R. Rail Yard known as Swift Current. In the hills of the prairies near the creek for which the town was named, partially obscured by prairie wool were strategically placed stones that would forever change her life. It was there that she went each day at sun down where she would sing a part of her spirit and wishes into stones and place them within the formation. It was an exercise in faith that the magic stones would take her home, far into the future. Timing was crucial.

Sunday after she sung the four stones into place, she admired her work and realised she was half way there.

One more week would see the completion of placing her stones within the Medicine Wheel and then maybe, just maybe, she could go home.

She felt inclined to rest and sit there awhile as though some invisible force was holding her. Strong feelings of longing for Derek threatened to overwhelm her. "Oh, Derek, I miss you so. I long to look into your eyes and feel your strong arms around me and tell you how much I love you and need you to be by my side." On the evening breeze in the light of the setting sun, she would have sworn she heard I love you. "Derek? Derek, can you hear me? Are you there, waiting for me? Oh please say that you are." Rim-Fyre nudged her off her seat on the rock and onto her hands and knees. Jumping up rapidly Serena turned to look at him. "What'd you do that for?" Stepping before her he offered his side, indicating that it was time to go back and call it a night.

Each evening since the fiasco at Thanksgiving dinner with family, Derek saddled Slade and rode out to the stones. He was positive it was an ancient Medicine Wheel. He rode for the partnership of the giant Canadian gelding and to get away from the house that reminded him that his wife was gone. He couldn't think there and he needed to be outside under the stars. That was where he did his best thinking. If wishing alone could have brought Serena to him, she would be here now in his arms. Had he done something to piss off the universe that it had taken his wife away?

Jess's research had provided enough information about Medicine Wheels to invoke a million more questions. The Indians didn't know what they were for umpteen years ago, and philosophers were calling it an enigma! Some enigma alright! He was damn sure his wife had disappeared here and yet he didn't know how or why. And for whatever reason this place and these rocks were like a magnet to him. Was she just here on the other side? How could he get there? What was the secret? Not knowing what else to do, Derek spent a half hour there, talking to Serena even though she couldn't hear him or see him. He could only hope that somehow his message got to her. And if nothing else, it helped him just to talk about life and all the problems he had encountered without her here. He wasn't sure if he could handle his wife being dead. Or maybe that would be better because then he would know without a doubt that she was never coming back. Derek still felt in his heart that Serena was still alive. They had a connection that was unlike anything he had ever experienced in his whole life. He loved her with every fiber of his being. "Serena, if you're there, I love you."

As the week wore on, the moon became fuller each night to cast its pale glow on the earth. Serena watched the sunset, hoping and praying that when she placed the stones tonight, that the following night was the true, full, Hunter's Moon. If she had missed it by a day or if it didn't work, she had no idea what she would do if she was stuck here in 1887. She did not want to plan her future here in the past. It was time to place the final stones. With four stones at the ready, she began her song and ended it with the same words, "… take me home, magic stones."

The sun slipped behind the western horizon and the moon rose in the east. It was big and it looked full, only one marred edge of the right side of the moon indicated that maybe it wasn't full yet. Tomorrow it would be and she could go home, finally.

Serena lingered longer this evening, sitting by the moonlight was comforting and she felt like she wasn't alone. It wasn't just Rim-Fyre but something else. Someone else, waiting … for her. "I love you, Derek. I have faith that it will be tomorrow." She said with confidence.

Rim-Fyre carefully picked his way back over the dry prairie grass, soon to be frozen to sleep for the winter. Serena could hear the geese, they too were gathering for a big migration. She could see the reflection of the moonlight on the water as she crossed it before making their way across the flat.

Rim-Fyre neighed a greeting. Serena recognized it as a friendly greeting and could make out two riders in the dark. The riders were not rushing but walking confidently toward her. A familiar voice called out, "Hey ho, Serena, it is me, Nawat Sinopa."

"Good evening, Nawat Sinopa, what brings you out here?" She asked wondering who his riding partner was. As they neared Serena could make out another familiar face in the light of the moon. "Peenaquim?"

Nawat Sinopa chuckled, "You sound surprised to see us. We have come to ask you to take tea with us at the village, Peenaquim has important news."

"Of course I would be honored to take tea with the great Medicine Man, Peenaquim." Serena bowed her head slightly to show her respect of the elder. She turned to Nawat Sinopa whose chiseled features caught the light of the moon, "Isn't your uncle too old to be riding that many miles on horseback?"

"I no old!" Peenaquim retorted.

Serena looked incredulous and Nawat Sinopa nearly fell off his horse laughing. Peenaquim joined him in laughter after seeing the expression on Serena's face. She had no choice but to laugh, too, it was contagious.

"Don't worry, it's the only English he knows." Nawat Sinopa added still chuckling.

They rode the mile to the little Indian village of seven tipis. A few fires burned brightly and sparked into the night sky. They dismounted at Nawat Sinopa's tipi and sat cross-legged at his fire. A pot of water was placed on the tripod and soon water was boiling for tea.

Peenaquim began to speak to Serena in his native tongue. She intently watched and listened to him, concentrating on his expressions and tone of voice while she could hear the English translation of Nawat Sinopa to her right. "Pelipa," she noticed he called her by her Spirit name. "I have made long journey because the Spirit Helpers came to me in a dream. My presence is requested by those far wiser than I. When the Hunter's Moon rises in the east I must sing you into the stones. I have come to fulfill my destiny so that you can fulfill yours."

Serena didn't understand why Peenaquim had to sing her home, too, but who was she to question the Spirits. "Thank you Peenaquim. I honor your presence here to assist me on my journey."

"Heya," he said smiling his toothless grin.

There was some small talk between Nawat Sinopa and Peenaquim which was translated to English for Serena's benefit and inclusion into the conversation.

This felt like the right time for Serena to present the gift she made to Nawat Sinopa. She cleared her throat, "Nawat Sinopa, before I go this night and see you on my last day here, I wish to present this gift to you in great appreciation for all that you have done for me since we first met." She took the little bundle out of her shirt pocket and set it in his hand. He accepted it gratefully.

Glancing at the little bundle, he knew what it was and represented. He could feel the power in the articles tied together with horse hair and gently closed his fingers around it. Nawat Sinopa looked up at Serena and for the first time, there was intense eye contact between them. She allowed him this once, the opportunity to peer into her soul for a few seconds. "Thank you, Serena. I will cherish this bundle all my days." Then he tucked the little bundle into his special leather pouch that hung around his neck, near his heart.

"Should I meet you at the stones tomorrow by sunset then?" She asked.

"Yes, we will meet you there." Nawat Sinopa answered for them both.

Serena stood and Rim-Fyre was ready and waiting to go. The moon shone high above them now as Serena bid them good night and rode off to what she hoped would be her last night's sleep in 1887.

NINETEEN
Hunter's Moon

Horses lend us the wings we lack.
~ Pam Brown

Mac gave his wife a kiss, "Enjoy your visit with Derek before he leaves, it might be a long time before any more relatives come to visit. I'll take Katie and we'll go to the Beckett's for a few hours."

Joan returned his kiss which promised more, later. "Thank you, Mac, you are a real sweetheart. I love you."

"I'll come back in time to say good-bye to Derek before he leaves." He gave her another kiss for good measure, scooped up the basket containing their sleeping daughter and walked out the door.

Serena tidied her room upstairs, making the bed and taking everything else downstairs with her. She changed into her own clean clothes this morning and tied the borrowed clothes together in a bundle to return to Joan. The only thing she was taking with her was the buffalo robe that Peenaquim gifted to her the first week she had been here. Dozens of times already she had used it to keep herself warm. It was also a beautiful reminder of the Buffalo Spirit that had come to speak to her. It sustained her the five weeks that she'd been here. Serena was sure that part of the buffalo's spirit was still in the robe for it was sacred and precious. The eagle wing feather was safely tucked inside her shirt. It, too, held a part of the eagle's spirit.

The women shared their thoughts, hopes and dreams over a pot of coffee and some pastries Joan saved for just this occasion. They laughed and almost cried and then laughed some more. The afternoon wore on in comfortable conversation as the women hadn't been able to visit much with daily chores and Serena working for the merchants. Serena's daily trips to the Medicine Wheel had also taken up a big chunk of her time.

"I'm going to miss you, Serena, even though you didn't want to be here, stuck in the past. I'm glad you came and that I had an opportunity to meet you." Joan expressed sincerely.

"I will miss you too Joan. You have become my very best friend. Without you, I would not have known where to turn or what to do. Is there any message you want me to take back to your family?" Serena asked.

"Yes, there is a message. Tell them to go to wherever they keep archives and look up the year 1887-88. I will find a way to leave them a message there so that they will know where I am and that I'm well and happy here."

"Alright, I can do that. Thank you, Joan, for everything and above all, for your friendship."

"You're welcome and thank you." Joan smiled.

"Well it's time to pack my horse and say all the good-byes that require saying. It's been hard but it's been a journey and experience I will always remember."

"Serena?"

"Yes, Joan," she said turning to make eye contact with her friend.

"I don't mean to discourage you in any way, but what if you don't go back to your time? What will you do then?"

Serena laughed, "Well, then I'll come back here and harass you for the rest of my life, that's what!"

Chuckling Joan shook her head, "I suppose you're right, there's no point in thinking that way, is there? You will go home to your Derek I'm sure."

Rim-Fyre was saddled and packed with her robe, she was ready to go. Final good-byes were said to Mac, Katie and Joan before she mounted her horse to head out.

"Your little horse will be the talk of these parts here for some time, Derek. We won't soon forget the Canadian. Take care, ride safe and write sometime!" Mac added as Serena waved one last time and turned to ride away.

Serena allowed Rim-Fyre to walk through the grass on their way up the hill to their vantage point from the cut-banks. As they neared the crest of the hill Serena could hear wild whooping and hollering coming from the Métis encampment down near the Roundhouse. Rim turned to look at what all the commotion was about when four riders came screaming around the closest tipi they could see, headed right for them.

Her stomach was already doing flip-flops from being anxious at the thought of going home but the sight of those riders flying toward them from across the valley sent adrenalin coursing down her legs. They were a threat to her getting home and there were only three and half miles between here and the Medicine Wheel. She knew that she would have to run Rim-Fyre farther than that to outdistance them and she sure didn't want them at the sacred site.

Instead of running, she waited and kept Rim-Fyre at a walk as they went across the top of the hill and perused the valley below. Maybe the Métis weren't after her to cause trouble after all. They were gaining on her as they ran their Indian ponies up the hill and toward her. Rim-Fyre spun beneath her to face them, on guard and ready to fight if necessary.

They sharply pulled up their ponies as they approached her. "Where ya think yer goin'?" The largest man of the group asked.

Alcohol wafted on the breeze and assailed her senses. "For a ride. Why are you bothering me?" She asked.

"Give us yer horse and nobody gets hurt." Said another with his hat askew.

Serena saw that two of the Métis had hand guns tucked into their belts and they all carried large skinning knives in sheaths on their belts. Rim was quite agitated already, Serena could feel it.

She had to think and act quickly. These men were drunk and perhaps they would give up or fall off their horses, she decided to make a run for it and hoped that if she needed it, Nawat Sinopa would be able to help her.

No spurs were necessary, Rim-Fyre was more than ready to make a break for it and as soon as Serena thought it, he leaped forward, front feet off the ground as he bumped into one of the Métis ponies shoving it off balance and running hell bent for leather.

She had no intentions of looking back but hoped that Rim caught them off guard enough to give them a few seconds head start. The whooping and hollering began and shots rang out. She laid herself flat against Rim-Fyre's neck, mane whipping in her face, as he galloped down the hill and across the valley. More shots were fired but Serena didn't hear any zing close by.

Rim ran as fast and straight as an arrow, knowing exactly where he was going. The gunfire ceased but Serena could still hear them whooping and galloping after them as fast as their ponies could go. Knowing she didn't have enough time to run for ten miles in order to lose them or for them to give up, she hoped Nawat Sinopa was already at the Medicine Wheel. Maybe he could hear all the hollering in the valley and would come to her rescue as they galloped over the next rise.

Never faltering once, Rim-Fyre ran true and sure, up a rise and down the hill and around the bend in the creek. They ran more than two miles and still the Métis bandits did not give up the chase.

'Oh Creator and Great Eagle Spirit, guide my horse and see me home.' Serena thought as Rim kept up his grueling pace. They were almost there. She had never run a horse flat out over this type of terrain for more than half mile let alone the two and a half they had already come. There were some small trees and brush along the creek, daylight was waning and the sun would

soon set. The moon would rise in the east. The Eagle Spirit said she only had a few minutes to pass through the portal on the Hunter's Moonrise.

If it was possible, Rim-Fyre burst forward even faster as the bandits continued their chase. Perhaps a little more distance would give them a chance of finding help. Rim-Fyre slowed to a lope as he approached the crossing in the creek where they crossed every day, then burst up the opposite bank and up the knoll to streak across the prairie again toward the sacred stones.

Serena spotted Nawat Sinopa's horse, saw him leap on her back with agility and speed and run toward them. They both stopped rapidly when they reached one another. Only then did Serena look back to where the bandits might be.

They were crossing the water at the creek and two of the ponies were refusing to go. The two bandits left their cohorts behind and were making their way toward Serena and Nawat Sinopa. No words were necessary as he realized the dangerous situation Serena had come across. His tomahawk at the ready he yipped and whooped and charged his mare straight at the Métis. Serena did not want him to face her foes alone. Her whip unslung from its tie and at the ready in her hand, Rim, too, charged forward to meet them.

The horses nearly smashed into each other as they met the two Métis and their ponies. Keeping her eye on which Métis Nawat Sinopa was going to grapple with, Serena set her sights on the other. Swinging her whip up and back down with a resounding C-R-A-C-K, right on his horse's velvety soft nose, the pinto horse reared in pain and surprise, catching the bandit off guard and clawing for air as he crashed onto his back on the ground. The horse ran off and now her opponent was trying to catch his drunken breath. Rim reared over him dominantly.

Serena quickly assessed the scene in which Nawat Sinopa was wrestling on the ground with the other Métis Before she could say or do anything, the other two bandits galloped over the knoll and into the fray. One of who was holding a loaded gun.

Serena turned Rim-Fyre toward the two Métis, coming up from the creek bank, she did not see Nawat Sinopa dispatch the drunk he was fighting with and yell "NO-O-O!!!!" behind her. The drunken man she faced fired off a shot. Nawat Sinopa ran past Rim-Fyre hurling his tomahawk with deadly accuracy at the shooter, hitting him square in the forehead. Serena saw the tomahawk hit the man and then doubled over in the saddle.

The bandit on the ground regaining his breath and the other drunken fool were making an advance to exact revenge for their buddy's deaths. The rider pulled a gun out of his belt and cocked the hammer. From out of nowhere, a buffalo three times the size of his horse ran him down, crushing his lifeless body into the prairie grass while his horse rolled up and ran off. A cougar screamed its attack and leaped upon the Métis who Serena knocked down earlier and with a quick snap of his neck, the would-be bandit was silently dragged off into the darkness.

It was eerily quiet now. Serena fell off Rim-Fyre holding her stomach before Nawat Sinopa had a chance to catch her. Peenaquim walked out of the bushes and over to them as Nawat Sinopa kneeled at her side and held her head up to a semi-sitting position. Blood oozed from between Serena's fingers as she held her stomach and grimaced in pain.

"No! This wasn't supposed to happen. I have to go home now." She cried.

The moon was just fully visible over the eastern horizon.

Nawat Sinopa looked into Peenaquim's eyes, "Uncle, we must care for her, she is too weak to go."

"No nephew, if she stays here she will die. If she goes, she lives. Come, we must put her on her Spirit Horse. He waits."

And he did. Rim-Fyre stood with the moon behind him, looking like a ghostly apparition outlined in the glow of the full moon. He stood stoic and proud waiting for his charge.

Serena saw him as she lay upon the ground, bleeding profusely with her guts on fire. Now more than ever she wanted to go home and she knew that Rim-Fyre would take her there. With renewed determination she pushed herself up with one hand. "Help me up, please."

Peenaquim and Nawat Sinopa helped her to stand by grabbing the crook of her elbows. Rim-Fyre walked into position so that Serena could reach up and grab the saddle horn. She placed her foot in the stirrup and Nawat Sinopa gently boosted her up so that she could swing her other leg over the saddle. Serena plunked her bottom in the saddle and hoped that Rim would forgive her this one time.

Peenaquim began walking to the sacred stones while Nawat Sinopa walked beside Rim-Fyre, holding Serena in the saddle so she wouldn't fall off.

"I just want to say thank-you, Nawat Sinopa, for saving my life, not once, but twice. I have to do this. Go home that is. It can't be any other way. May the Eagle Spirit always fly with you."

Peenaquim stood at the 12 o'clock position of the sacred stones while the moon climbed ever higher in the sky, it was orange and full, casting a glow on the land.

"Ride with the Spirits, Serena." He said placing his hand over hers for a brief moment.

Rim-Fyre and Serena were a few horse lengths before the pathway into the sacred stone circle facing Peenaquim. Nawat Sinopa smiled at her and walked away.

Peenaquim began to sing, and so it began. "Heya, heya, heya, hey …"

Serena gripped her knees onto Rim-Fyre's sides, ready to ride despite the gnawing pain in her stomach from the bullet wound. He loped slowly from a standstill carrying his charge as carefully as he possibly could. One stride, two strides, three and entry into the path of the stone circle. Peenaquim's voice chanting "heya", then Rim-Fyre jumped into the circle over the invisible barrier only he could see. To Peenaquim and Nawat Sinopa it appeared as though the horse and rider leapt into a ring of fire and disappeared as the gifted buffalo robe fell to the ground.

TWENTY
Home

To ride a horse is to ride the sky.
~ Author Unknown

"I'm going for a walk. I'll be back in an hour or so." Derek said to his kids as he dressed to go outside.

"Can I come, dad?" Cole asked.

"No, buddy, I need to be by myself and think about life. Maybe we'll play a game of chess when I get back, okay?"

"Al-right," came out, in a rejected tone.

Derek discovered a shortcut over the course of the past few weeks from the farm house to the location of the Medicine Wheel. The sun was still setting and the moon wasn't out yet. It was the full moon and he was restless. Along the creek bank south of the house he walked, using the beautiful walking stick Cole gave him the previous Christmas. He walked not more than a quarter mile to where there was an island in the creek. A deer trail led down to the water, a few feet of shallow water separated the island, there the trail continued through the willows and onto the other side. Rocks stuck out of the shallow water that he used as stepping stones to get to the other side of the creek. From that point he could walk about a mile to the Medicine Wheel.

Derek walked with purpose and was able to walk to the stones within a half hour. It felt right for him to be in this place, right now. He sat on one of the larger rocks in the circle of stones in the waning light of the sunset so that he could watch the moon crest and rise in the east.

His wife had been missing for five long weeks with nary a sign of her anywhere. Where on earth could she be? Derek decided that he would wait until hell froze over if he had to, until he found his wife dead or alive.

He sat there quietly listening to the sounds of the night on the prairie and watched the moon gradually make its appearance in the night sky. The moon seemed larger and more pronounced watching it from this vantage point this evening than he could ever remember having seen it before. From the time it first came into view until the entire moon was visible was only several minutes by the clock. It shone brightly and in the light of the Hunter's Moon, Derek made a wish.

Derek's hair stood up on the back of his neck when a blinding light flashed behind him, followed by hoof beats and a long wet snort. He jumped up and whipped around to see a horse and rider in the moonlight. "What the ..."

When Rim-Fyre jumped into the sacred circle of stones, Serena saw only a bright flash then they landed and came to an abrupt standstill. Serena looked down and felt her stomach, then took her hand away. There was no blood and no burning sensation in her abdomen at all. She looked up to see someone standing at the foremost stone before them. It wasn't Peenaquim chanting. Where was she now?

Serena asked tentatively, "Who's there?"

The moonlight lent itself to lighting enough of the darkness for Derek to make out a horse he hadn't seen in some time. The shaky voice was familiar, "Serena? Is that you?"

"Derek?"

"Serena!"

"Derek!" With one swift swing-jump, Serena's feet were on the ground and she was running for her husband whose outstretched arms reached for her as they came together in a fierce embrace.

Rim-Fyre bugled his return to the herd in the distance, their reply echoing through the valley.

Happy tears were rolling down their cheeks as they hugged, pulling back at arms-length to look at each other, to assure themselves that this was real. "I love you." They said in unison.

"I have a million questions, Serena, and so much to tell you. But no matter what, I love you and I'm so glad you're home."

Serena wiped her eyes on the back of her sleeve. "What I'm about to tell you is going to be pretty unbelievable. Oh I missed you!" She said hugging him again.

"It would be harder for me to believe if I wasn't here just now when you came back. I've had some wild things happen here, too. I would believe pretty much anything right about now." He shook his head.

"Hang on a sec," Serena broke the embrace and walked toward Rim-Fyre who was still standing in the center of the circle. Gently stroking his face she whispered for him only. "Thank you for bringing me home. Now let's go."

Serena held one rein and began walking back to Derek. The first step that Rim took produced a clink in the grass. It sounded funny so she stopped him and bent to see what he hit in the grass with his hoof. She brushed the grass around and uncovered a tin-like object. Rim knocked it loose by hitting it, so she picked it up to hold it in the light. "No way!" she said, "It can't be."

Derek strode over to her to see what she found. "What can't be? What is that?"

"This," she said holding it so he could see, "is my stainless steel coffee mug."

He took it from her hand and inspected it. The plastic lid was nearly chewed off by rodents, only bits of the plastic outer rim remained and the stainless interior and outside of the mug rusted and thin. "It looks like it's been out here for a hundred years."

"125 actually." Serena said looping her arm into the crook of his elbow. "Let's go home and I'll tell you all about it."

Serena told Derek all about her wild adventures on Rim as they walked back to the farm in the moonlight. Holding hands most of the way.

Before they walked into the barn, Derek stopped her. Tossing her hat in the barn, he held her cheeks in his hands and gave her a deep, slow kiss, followed by several quick kisses all over her face. "I've been waiting for over five weeks to do that." He said chuckling.

Rim-Fyre rubbed his head against the couple so they wouldn't forget he was there. This produced more laughter from both of them. "We better put him in his corral."

Back in his pen and after the chorus of whinnied greetings subsided, Rim went to quietly eat his hay.

Derek and Serena sat on the bench outside their barn in the moonlight holding hands. They shared the bulk of their experiences the past month, knowing that once they got to the house the kids were going to be all over their mom, peppering her with questions.

After greeting her children and telling them enough of her story to appease them, they went to their rooms for the night.

She languished in the shower until the water ran cold. So grateful for everything she had, family, home and an amazing horse.

Derek made tea while she was in the shower. Holding her tea, she stood at the patio window overlooking the creek, at the high moon casting its reflective gaze on the water. Derek came up behind and wrapped his arms around her waist, breathing in her soft womanly scent at her neck. "I'm glad you're home. I missed you like crazy."

Serena held the eagle's wing feather to her heart, closing her eyes, she whispered, "Heya." Gently she laid the feather on the bedside table before she got into bed and snuggled into her husband's waiting arms.

Rim-Fyre gazed at the Hunter's Moon. They were better bonded mentally and spiritually for the experience. He had accomplished what he set out to do. The next leg of the journey would have to wait until his offspring were born and the Hay Moon arrived. It was going to be a long winter.

Acknowledgements

Thank you to my friends Sandra Rowe and Mary White, and my sister-in-law, Wanda, for your unfailing moral support and encouragement. Writing a fiction story is a hard but worthwhile experience. I appreciate your feedback on my story. I can hardly wait to go riding with you!

My biggest fans and supporters are those who went the extra mile in promoting my first published work, HOOF PRINTS ON MY HEART. Thanks also to Mom and Mylan. I love you both so much!

Sheila Steinley, once again you captured a photo worthy of the cover of a book - mine! Thank you! Many thanks to Heather Upchurch from Expert Subjects for making Sheila's photo extraordinary and for your patience in helping to "see" my vision for this cover. It was a pleasure to work with you.

I have a great deal of appreciation for Glenda Fordham for proofreading my manuscript and giving positive and valuable feedback on this story. Thanks Glenda!

Once again, my husband Darren is worthy of the "Husband of the Year Award". Without his unfailing love and support, feeding our horses while I was sick in January, taking care of me and bringing me Tim Horton's while I was hospitalized with pneumonia. "Thank you Honey, I love you and couldn't do it without you."

I am inspired by the Canadian horse, my home land of Saskatchewan, Canada, and the hope for a brighter tomorrow.

Without God, the Creator and Great Spirit I am nothing. I am grateful. ~Amen

Made in the USA
Charleston, SC
19 May 2013